Emails from Heaven

An angel's advice to his

young apprentice.

By Matt Rawlins

Emails from Heaven by Matt Rawlins.

OTHER BOOKS
BY MATT RAWLINS

Rediscovering Reverence, the Path to Intimacy

Humility

Walking Naked into the Land of Uncertainty

The Question

The Namer

The Container

Mysteries Beyond the Gate &
other peculiar short stories

The Guardian

LEADERSHIP BOOKS FOR THE MARKETPLACE

BY MATT RAWLINS

The Green Bench
A dialogue about Leadership and Change

The Green Bench II
Ongoing dialogue about Leadership and Communication

Emails from Hell

The Lottery
A question can change a life

There's an Elephant in the Room
Discover the single most power tool for growth

Finding the Pain in your @ss-umption
A Leadership Tale

Managing Presence in the Midst of Tension
Five core leadership skills

Introduction

I've seen hundreds of pictures of angels, but I can't remember ever hearing a sermon about them. There are 273 mentions of angels in the Bible. They are God's messengers. Others are warriors and worshippers. That's about all we know. I propose there is a training class of those who want a head start on learning how they work with us as we will one day rule over them.

I must admit I knew almost nothing about angels until I found these emails. I was astonished to discover they are much more involved in our everyday lives than we realize. As His messengers, they speak to us often, trying to train us in the ways of God. But we are not good listeners. These emails are an attempt to make it clearer for those of us who have a hard time listening.

I cannot say how I came into possession of these documents, but I admit they were a gift. They unveil to me -- and now you -- the mystery of how angels work among us and what they are trying to teach us about the Kingdom of God.

A Pilgrim at The Portal

Insight@heaven.edu
Whisper@heaven.edu
Subject: The arrival

Dear Whisper,

By now you will have arrived, and I am sure
nothing I said or could have said would have
prepared you for your work in their dark and
desperate world. We have no references like it
here. The closest we come to understanding it
is when the unfaithful one comes to rant, rave and
parade before the throne of The Sovereign One.
Some younger angels' wretch whenever he
appears. Thankfully, the sweet pure air of
Heaven quickly removes his foul stench.

Down there, the unfaithful one's stench is found in
everything, I am sure it will take some getting
used to for you. As I mentioned before, I will
stay in constant contact with you as keeping
your bearings will be difficult. I will try and
simplify the ideas so as they make sense in the
chaotic and dark world you're now in.

Remember your work is to prepare for a
visitation from Our Beloved Father. Your work
is vital to His purpose as without some form of
foundation built in their lives, the effects of His
Visitation would be like pouring water into the
desert. It would be quickly consumed but have
very little long-term effect.

Begin to observe your honor bearer that was assigned to you and give me an assessment of what is happening.

In the King's service,
Insight

Insight@heaven.edu
Whisper@heaven.edu
Subject: Your honor bearer

Dear Whisper,

The new feelings within you are normal. Your description of a crystal-clear river that has been muddied is a good one. The power of evil hides and muddies everything. I am sure by now you've become aware of the challenge it is just to think clearly. Ideas, words and their meanings are the battleground there. They are also the tools you use to think with and thus it is hard work to think clearly in the presence of evil.

I am glad you ask about the meaning of 'honor bearer' as now that you are there and have your eyes on him, it will take on new meaning.

Honor is a simple term linked to glory. In this case our Beloved's glory.

Bearer is one who carries on behalf of another. Often a servant who bears the responsibility of carrying things of value for their leader.

So, in the case of humanity, a man or woman, made in the image of our Beloved, who is restored to a relationship with Him through Jesus. They now carry the honor of the Son and look to bear His image through their life.

I am glad you have great joy in finding and observing your honor bearer. It is a mystery and a joy to know that one day they will rule over us. It is our greatest pleasure to work with and serve them as Our Exalted Father prepares them for that day.

Thank you for the details of your honor bearer. He is a teacher, so we are in a similar vocation. I am glad he loves to read, even though it seems to be a lost art for many of them. His recent marriage will be a great opportunity for him to learn a lot about himself and the essence of love in a dark world. His desire to 'work out' and exercise is good for his body, but it can be a distraction, as in all things, we shall see soon enough.

Remember, in the nature of our work, we are not focused on their culture or the church they attend. Frankly it is irrelevant to us as we go beneath it. Our work is to deal with issues of the heart that are common to all honor bearers. What you discover about your work with him will enable you to understand any honor bearer, regardless of age, gender or nationality. Yes, he is young in his faith, but do not discount that, it is a key time to do the foundational work needed for the long-term health of him and his family.

In the King's service,
Insight

PS. (I find myself also at times referring to them as dust creatures. Let me state the obvious as to why I do this, they are living beings, formed from the dust with the breath of our Beloved in them.)

Insight@heaven.edu
Whisper@heaven.edu
Subject: Selfishness is a mystery

Dear Whisper,

You are right. I am sure it is not difficult for you to see where the confusion is for them in their values and thus in making wise choices. I particularly like your description of this and the question you raise.

> My honor bearer and his old college friends desire things that are unimaginable outside of this dark place. For instance, they seem preoccupied to find the right clothes. They shop to get just the right design with the right label on it so that others will see the clothes as valuable. I have found him looking in a mirror at his stringy black hair and dark eyes and then trying to match clothes to 'the look'. He and his buddies have no idea that they were never even made to wear clothes or coverings. They are a result of their own foolish rebellion and when they finally are free from their world, they will also be free from their coverings.
>
> I cannot imagine why they do not want Our Beloved? As you so

wisely wrote, is He not the most unique, beautiful, quality and needed being in the universe?

You have started off our correspondence by bringing up a mystery. It is an excellent question that goes deep. I assume that in your thinking, if you could just figure out the mystery, you think you could really help them. Let me say right up front, it doesn't work like that. Even Our Beloved Father gives us an awareness that He does not understand the mystery of sin. He wrote in one of His love letters to them and asked, 'Why when I planted good grapes did it produce evil....'' Selfishness is a mystery I am afraid. If the Almighty doesn't understand why, then we cannot either (see note below).

It is not rational, but it does have its own perverse logic. They now assume they are animals, defined by natural instincts. Things which Our Beloved gave them for intimacy and beauty, have been turned into a lust for sex, food, possessions and fashion. As one of our Beloved's servants wrote so well, 'They are content with mud pies when a banquet hall with a feast has been prepared for them.'

Your work is to awaken the image of Our Beloved in him. Then and only then will he realize he is so much more than an animal.

In the King's service,
Insight

(I know my statement above about Our Beloved 'not understanding the mystery of sin' will not make sense. Our Beloved has infinite understanding about all things, but He also tells us it is a mystery or enigma to Him. I have talked with Him about it, but He smiles and says it will take time for us to grow into the revelation of what He means. I carry the tension of it with great anticipation and faith, which only means there are greater and deeper mysteries ahead for us of which I cannot wait for the day to come.)

Whisper@heaven.edu
Insight@heaven.edu
Subject: He asks questions

Dear Whisper,

Your honor bearer sounds interesting. His struggle with the kids in his class will give you lots of opportunities to understand him better. Find the spark in him and watch over it. Let me be as clear as I can about this: Don't worry about the unfaithful one or any of his minions there. Let the warriors do the battle, and of course he will have to do the battle as well. Your primary role is to nurture the spark within him. We are trainers. Build the spark into a fire that warms all those around him.

Our Beloved gave them wisdom right after the rebellion and it will serve you well to remind him of the insight given to them. When Adam and Eve turned from our Beloved, He asked them three questions. Let me put words to this glorious revelation of His humility.

The Sovereign One, the One Before All things and who is without End, starts his interaction with these little rebels by asking questions. What they heard and responded to was not great revelation to them, but it caused a wave of worship here in heaven.

When I AM is near us, when we sense His presence more clearly, an overriding sense of awe fills us. Imagine reaching out with your finger and 'touching' eternity. Not becoming eternal but touching a 'cell' of it. You are filled with a sense that HE KNOWS. He is infinite wisdom, pure and without end. No one can counsel Him or give Him wisdom. He knows it all, from quantum mechanics to the weight of the universe.

And YET, His first response to the rebels was to ask questions.

In their darkened world, humanity expects the Sovereign One to ask questions as if their opinion really matters. How arrogant of them to think they can counsel Our Beloved or give Him anything He doesn't already know or have.

To watch Him who is Before all things, ask questions of humanity, I tell you, we were undone. We talked about it all the way up to the highest circles of light. It had never entered our mind that the I AM could humble Himself in such a way. It was pure genius, extravagant humility combined with extended grace. He used a question to invite, to create more space for them, even in their flagrant hiding from His presence, He pursued them.

In light of this, we must assume that one of the most powerful tools you can give to your honor bearer is freedom to ask questions. Encourage him to be curious about life and to explore it as a child does.

Don't let him think that all questions must be answered on the spot. That is such a narrow focus. Encourage him that some questions he will have to grow into and may take years, glorious years of growth, to 'know' the answer. This curious thirst is vital to long term growth and insight into the ways of Our Beloved.

As a brief side note, the unfaithful one used the appearance of questions for his own devious end, 'Indeed, has God said...?'. He knew the power of them and gave the appearance of a question, though it was really a hidden accusation. He is always trying to steal the ways of Our Beloved for his own foolishness.

In the King's service,
Insight

Whisper@heaven.edu
Insight@heaven.edu
Subject: The first question

Dear Whisper,

I am so glad to hear of the hunger your honor
bearer has. As I said in the last email, continue
to fuel this hunger with curiosity. It is really
two sides of the same coin as they say. His
marriage will force him to look outside of
himself for answers and his faith will draw
him to our Beloved. You don't say anything
about his wife, and it seems you assume all
marriages are the same. I hope this is not your
thinking as each marriage is so very different.
Their reactions to each other, how they support
or feed off each other or just the foundations of
their marriage and what drew them together
all create a unique interaction. I know your
focus is on him but be aware of her as it is the
spouse that often provides the richest
opportunities to understand your honor bearer.
The richest and closest loves in the family
expose the deepest issues of the heart.

Now in regard to questions, the first question
Our Beloved asked, "Where are you?" is the
starting point for all life in a broken world.
Their break from reality in listening to the
unfaithful one was the starting point of this
struggle.

For those of us who have not drunk of the
deceit of the unfaithful one, we are drawn to reality
in all things. It is in our very essence as angels.

Your honor bearer is now in a radically different place, torn with the desire for reality and yet, terrified of it. Our Father begins with the first question to remind humans that an honest, acknowledgement of where they are is the starting place for walking into a deeper reality.

What is so simple to us at the deepest heart level, is now a life challenge for them. If Our Beloved were to reveal the reality of where they are, it would be judgment and they would be undone. So graciously, He allows them to grow into this reality over time. As he studies The Word, have him realize that Paul went from viewing himself as "the least of the Apostles" to "the worst of all sinners. He saw the reality of his heart more clearly with time. It takes time for the reality of the dark world and who they really are to be understood.

You must be aware and work with your honor bearer, true spirituality for them is not the absence of reality, it is a growing revelation of the pain of reality. Don't be surprised if they groan at times. Their reality is always with them. We can hear nature's groan in their dark world even from here.

They have little idea of the darkness they are in. And with this I struggle to even describe because, by its very definition, they can't see it. Like a sleeping man trying to understand being awake, they might catch a glimpse of it in a dream, but until they wake, they do not even know they are asleep. So, when they see light, only then can they begin to understand darkness.

It might help your honor bearer to understand deception by using the metaphor that it is a 'current', it is arrogance and lies against the reality of who Our Beloved is. Here, there is a current that flows naturally towards the center of the universe, reality. It flows to the very heart of Our Beloved. However, in their world, there is a constant current away from Our Beloved. If you don't fight it, you will naturally be drawn away from reality.

Our Wise One left that 'current' there so that the little ones would learn to fight it. It is only in fighting it that they grow their muscles of faith. We grow our faith because we have direct access to the light. They grow their faith by fighting against the current of darkness there. As long as they are in the body, they will have to swim against the currents of the world. There are no other options.

In the King's service,
Insight

Whisper@heaven.edu
Insight@heaven.edu
Subject: Science and faith

Dear Whisper,

I'm glad you asked the science question, and because your honor bearer is a science teacher, it is all the more relevant for him. It seems to be a growing contention in their dark world and something we need to stay current with. I wanted to get off a quick response to look at science and his faith before we look at the other questions our Beloved asks.

Your honor bearer assumes reality is science (which really means the material world). Therefore, he will feel a conflict between faith and science. The unfaithful one has worked hard to create this split, and we can see the bitter fruit of this lie all around. Your job is not to challenge his lies. There are just too many variations to know them all. You must keep your honor bearer focused on the truth. Reality starts in the heart of our Beloved.

Help your honor bearer see that science is quite useful in identifying all the organisms and natural forces. The Chief Scientist created life. Science tells them the 'what' of the amazingly complex world they inhabit. It also explains what happens when they do something. 'In this situation, at this time, I did … and this is what happened.' It is a question the mind was made to answer.

The deeper question is 'why'. The purpose, meaning or value behind the what. This is the question the heart must answer. It calls into question the value of something and gives you understanding of the motive in which to act.

They are not in opposition to each other. They were made to serve and honor each other.

Let me go back a step to my previous email. The first question, 'Where are you?', has to do with context. Meaning, reality can only be described in a context. It is not a snap shot of a moment, but in a story being told, where are you in 'this story of life'.

Materialists say humans evolved into who they are. To them, the 'Where are you? question is evolutionary. From Our Beloved's reality, it is more a question of relationship. Where are you in regard to Our Beloved and His creation?

In the King's service,
Insight

Whisper@heaven.edu
Insight@heaven.edu
Subject: The second question

Dear Whisper,

I know you want your honor bearer to be responsible, but it is not time yet to focus on that. In the air there, there is a lot of talk about responsibility, but you must work your way to it carefully. Words mean different things there than here. This word 'responsibility' is one of them. As we stand before our Beloved, we don't even use the word here as you do there.

As I look out my window, down into the park, I see angels coming and going and new arrivals from earth catching up with old friends. No one is hurrying, but each is busy with the expressions in their heart. I assure you, not one of them is worried about being irresponsible. Yet, that is a fear that often drives people in the world where you are.

My dear Whisperer, don't get caught up in their frantic life. When broken humans use this word, they are usually talking about the law, being right, earning their place or getting points to offset their wrong choices. Don't focus on responsibility…yet.

The second question will make this clearer.

'Who told you were you naked?'

I can remember the exact moment we angels watched them eat the fruit. All I can say is we were undone. The warriors picked up their swords and wanted to go to war. Others wept at such a blatant choice. Others stood, stunned, as they saw the look of sadness on our Beloved's face. Once you have seen that, you would do anything to never ever see such a sight again. It pierced us to the depths of our being.

I am sorry, I digress, I know these images will have grown faint and hard to remember in the air there. The very air there is set up to distort and twist the images of a good God. It seems the type of 'spell' cast by sin is an attack on the character of God, but more of that later. Trust me when I say that what you struggle to remember there, we can see in high definition here. The character of God enlightens like nothing else in the universe can.

This second question is about authority and listening. To whom is your honor bearer listening? You must help him to clarify who has authority to speak to him. Guide him to those who will be able to reinforce the story of his life.

This story is vital because the story of life clarifies the context for how they should live. It describes the ebb and flow of what is important, and they take it to heart and want to be in that story. Stories say who belongs, who is noticed, who is inside and who is outside. The story is vital to how they live.

Here is why I have encouraged you not to worry about responsibility yet. If he is responsible to the wrong story and is listening to the wrong authority, then all the responsibility in the world will not help him. Teach him that as an honor bearer, made in the image of our Beloved, one of his primary roles in life is to listen. Just as a child must tune their ear to their father and mother, so an honor bearer must turn their heart to our Beloved.

On a side note, the word they often use down there is obedience. It means to listen. We never use that word here. It makes no sense to us. We always give our Beloved our full attention. We listen for any hint of His desire and then rush to meet it. But this will not make sense to your honor bearer. Such attentiveness is foreign to him. Don't let your young honor bearer become caught up in being responsible and therefore obedient. Focus on love, listening to the Beloved, and he will do fine.

In the King's service,
Insight

Whisper@heaven.edu
Insight@heaven.edu
Subject: The third question

Dear Whisper,

You have stated well in your interpretation of
the last email. The question of authority is
understood in the sense of whom he is trying
to please. The person he is trying to please is
the one he has given authority to. This can be
rooted in fear (I please you so you don't hurt
me), or love (I please you because I value you).
It is not easy to distinguish these two areas in a
dark world. But with time you will learn how
to.

We all know what you are going through down
there. We have a love / hate relationship with
the dark planet. It has caused such grief in our
Beloved and yet, He has used it for such
revelation of who He is that we stand in awe of
Him. We hate the lies and arrogance of the
place. The smell of it is nauseating to us. But
knowing we are helping His children is joy
beyond our wildest dreams. Like you, we all
go to work there carrying the tension of this
conflict.

Only now can we look at the third question our
Beloved asks, 'Have you eaten from the tree of
which I commanded you not to eat?'

Only when there is an honest acceptance of
where they are, only after you have clarified
who they are listening to, then and only then

can they truly understand what they have done.

Remember what our Beloved made absolutely clear to them. There are no grey lines, no doubts or misunderstanding. He specified what they could not do and that is what He held them responsible for.

I write this because shame has now become a part of them. They 'use' responsibility to keep shame in its place, again, a misunderstanding of responsibility.

Strictly speaking, all they are responsible for is faith. Everything else is not something they initiate, but something that grows out of them in response to the overwhelming grace of our Beloved.

We must not shame them or belittle them in any way. The reality of life will do that for them. The focus of your job is simple. We want them to own their choices.

He will fight you on this, oh, like a fish on a hook, he will look for a thousand ways to get off it to have his 'freedom'. (He will consider responsibility just as a fish considers a hook - something others are trying to impose on him). Remember, freedom in their language is the absence of consequences. It is the idea that they may live however they want with no responsibility for the ripple effects of their choices. This loss of ownership of their life choices is the essence of darkness.

Choices are an expression of the internal. That is why transparency, vulnerability and honesty are so clearly vital to all of life here. Do not forget, that whenever Jesus shows up, there is a sacred awe in seeing His new physical body. He is the very heart (choice) of God on display. We know that when we see Him, we see the very heart of God walking in our midst.

That standard of choice, vulnerability, transparency is the standard of the kingdom and how all choices work here. The most natural thing in heaven is to know the heart of the person and realize their choices are a perfect representation of their heart.

Your honor bearer will not understand this as he has no sense of it being possible because of all he has experienced there. Your work is to slowly, very slowly, help him to walk into it. If necessary, go back to the start and remind him of these three questions:

Where are you? An honest, vulnerable acknowledgement of the reality of life. Both internally and externally.

Who told you...? An awareness of who has authority to tell the story of life and what part we play in it. Who is he listening to?

Have you eaten...? The importance of choice and learning to own his choices and the consequences of them.

All things can only grow in the light and there is so little light there. Thus, life grows slowly on that planet. Don't worry, that which does grow is hardy and worthy of life. Don't be tempted to compare growth here in the light and growth there in darkness. They have no idea of how fruitful and joyous growth is here. But one day, they will discover it and oh the joy that awaits them. I get excited just thinking of the pleasures that await your honor bearer.

In the King's service,
Insight

Whisper@heaven.edu
Insight@heaven.edu
Subject: What is true here, is a struggle there.

In your last note to me, you sounded surprised at what your honor bearer struggles with. Maybe shocked would be a better word. You mentioned the foul language of the kids in his class, his own role in helping them and his constant thinking about and struggling with finances with his wife. I think it is safe to say after a while down there, very little will shock you. What we take for granted here, is the very essence of their struggle there. Your work is to take the simplest and most basic things -- matters we don't think about for a second here -- and to get them to think about them there.

Let me give you the purest example, which will be your greatest struggle there with your honor bearer. His struggle, the reason it is dark there, is because he does not know who God is. It is not that he can't, but a good portion of his life was spent fighting the light. All his 'muscle' memory is against the light. Therefore, all his atrophied muscles must be developed anew.

I am not sure if you can remember watching when the unfaithful one was allowed access to the garden and spoke to Eve. We all stood on the edge of heaven, for we were not allowed to go down and be involved.

I still remember it as if it was yesterday; the unfaithful one declared in pompous arrogance to Eve, "You surely will not die." We looked at one another in astonishment. Some of us wanted to laugh because we thought it was a joke. Most of us turned to our Beloved and expected Him to defend Himself. What the unfaithful one said (without saying out loud), was that our Beloved was selfish. He could not speak it out for Eve would have laughed at him. So, he implied that our Beloved was holding back from her. That our Beloved did not have her highest in His heart and was not giving her what she deserved. Even to write such statements now hurts, my hand wants to revolt for putting such words down.

The unfaithful one called God a liar. Can you imagine such a statement spoken here? That thought never entered our mind, not once in a million years, and yet, he implied it as naturally as if he was commenting on the weather. Any one of us watching would have rushed down there to defend Him, but we felt His hand over our heart, whispering to us, 'Do not worry, I feel your desire to defend and cherish it, but this is their test and they must walk through it.'

The unfaithful one's strategy is ruthlessly simple, he attacks the character of God and implies that our Beloved is not good, righteous, merciful, longsuffering or patient. He cares about nothing else but destroying the character attributes of God and filling their mind with whom we know the unfaithful one to be. In a strange twist of light, the unfaithful one implies

32

that our Beloved cannot be trusted. He takes his own attributes (jealous, arrogant, indifferent, cruel, harsh or conceited) and then tries to convince the world that God is like that.

Help your honor bearer to realize this is The Strategy. His very life depends on who he thinks God is. He will struggle with this every day of his life in that dark world. His faith is not in religion, but in the very goodness and greatness of God. It is an active trust in who our Beloved says He is and not the lies about God that invade every strain of their broken life on the dark planet.

This false concept of who God is has worked its way into every aspect of their lives. They question our Beloved's honor as if it is the most natural thing in the world. Where we speak His name in the most awe inspired reverence here, these broken rebels will often use his name as a curse, judgment, or just to express displeasure.

We would rather call on the mountains to fall on us and crush us than say one sentence about God as they do; they do it as easily as a blind man speaks of the light or a deaf man of sound.

If our Beloved can allow them to continue in their current place, then we must trust Him and learn to bear them despite their utter arrogant blindness.

In the King's service,
Insight

Whisper@heaven.edu
Insight@heaven.edu
Subject: Is God good?

Dear Whisper,

You wisely ask, "How could they believe our
Beloved is not good?"

Don't waste any energy trying to figure out
'why' they believe the lies against our Beloved.
It is what I believe Paul wrote as the 'Mystery
of lawlessness'.

Evil (attacks against the character of God), is a
mystery. I am guessing that is why it is called
darkness or deception. Because you are in a
dark world, they will argue that there needs to
be a reason, that our Beloved must defend
Himself and tell them why there is evil in the
world. The mystery of wickedness is that there
is no reason for it, but don't get into that
argument with your honor bearer. The
assumption is that God needs to justify
Himself. We know clearly here that when we
see Him and His transparency, we know
instantly that He is who He says He is. This
argument is the fruit of their dark world and
the only way they can overcome it is through
faith in who He says He is. If they will not take
Him at His word, darkness has a hold on their
heart.

In a strange twist of thinking, they use this as
the basis of refusing to trust Him. They will

argue that because there is injustice, they cannot trust God. Notice again the foolishness of their thinking. They assume there is justice in the universe (only a just God could sustain that or give that idea to them) and then say because there is injustice, they will not believe in God.

If there was no God, injustice would have no meaning to them, but they are often just looking for an excuse in order to defend their brokenness. Remember, what makes perfect sense to us here, they will struggle with there.

For instance, this idea of light, they assume light is an idea, they assume it is abstracted truth in the sense that it is separate from life. Once they are enlightened, they will see the truth as separate from all things, they almost imagine it as if it exists on its own (Some will even call it a force). They are prepared to bow down to this abstracted truth and acknowledge it, but it is separate from God.

As you know well, here, our light is not abstract, it is relational. When I walk out and greet one of our friends, I am greeting the 'truth', as they are living it and truth is truth because it is lived in us. Truth or light is not something separate from us or even something separate from our Beloved. Our Father is truth, He IS light. It is His presence in a relationship that brings awareness, understanding and insight.

The unfaithful one will try and get your honor bearer to study 'truth' as an abstracted thought, separate from the self. Your work is to get him to study God in the sense that truth cannot be separated from a relationship. It is something that is lived, shared and experienced in and through love.

In the King's service,
Insight

Whisper@heaven.edu
Insight@heaven.edu
Subject: Shame

Dear Whisper,

I found your latest update on his infatuation with himself very funny. His preoccupation with his hair, his clothes, his tan and the size of his muscles, we laughed as a group as we remembered humans' zeal for how they look. Your description of him using gel to make his hairy look 'messed up' but working each hair into 'place' was hilarious. Although a 'surface' issue, it does expose roots that are very deep in their heart.

This goes back to the rebellion. They are now consumed with physical appearances rather than character. They assume they must be like God in nature. Remember when the unfaithful one seduced Eve with the idea that God was selfish? Then he changed focus and declared, "You will be like God…"

Now the reality of it was she was already like God. But we know the unfaithful one was not confirming what God already did but was trying to twist her thinking. To take her natural desire to be like God in character and to get her to assume she should be like God in His nature.

Again, notice the inference, the unfaithful one would not say it out loud for it would be laughed at by anyone who heard it. He implied she should be like God in nature.

The absurdity of this is beyond words. It has created a burden on them that is beyond our ability to comprehend. They now assume they must be like the Infinite One in His power, glory and greatness. These poor little creatures of dust feel the weight of this lie every day of their lives.

This has produced a shame in them that is like a cancer. They feel their limitations as inadequacy. Their utter inability to live up to this standard produces an embarrassment that is slowly killing them. It is why they fear and truly hate weakness.

Oh, that they might rediscover the joy of being finite. It is not a cause for shame, but a joy that gives opportunity to reveal new and greater things about our Beloved. Those who embrace their finite nature begin to realize that the greater the darkness, the more clearly they can see the light. They learn new things in their dark world that a million years here could not teach them. You are given an opportunity to be a part of that. It brings chills to me just to remind us of His glory and how we play a part in it.

In the King's service,
Insight

(Let me be extra clear here. Guilt is the feeling they have for their own wrong choices. His struggle with pornography in the past will try to bring guilt into his life. He has sought forgiveness and received it completely from Jesus. However, what often happens is shame then feeds off the past guilt and his struggle amplifies from 'I did something wrong' to 'I am wrong'. You will notice here that he can't 'repent' of being an honor bearer because he didn't choose it. Shame is a 'false' guilt for being alive.)

Whisper@heaven.edu
Insight@heaven.edu
Subject: Problems vs Dilemmas

Dear Whisper,

I agree, they are simplistic, naïve and desire to reduce everything to a problem they can solve. His annoyance with his wife and then trying to 'fix' her (and the argument that followed) was an excellent example. Welcome to the human race. You have stated your challenge so simply that I will want to use it in my work with other angels.

The issue of making everything a problem to be solved is so foreign to us here, but it's something you must recognize.

Here in The City, we clearly see diversity all around us. Life here is full of dilemmas. There are so many choices of equal value and beauty, so many opportunities of reveling in the grace of our Beloved and expressing it in unique ways. In all these choices, we have no fear, only anticipation. We know any choice we make in Him is His greatest joy.

We are not concerned about doing the right thing, because we know we are right. Not in what we do, but in who we are. This natural, overflowing joy is so much a part of life, it seems as natural and normal as the River of Life here.

Now to contrast this with their dark world, where they assume, they are wrong in their very existence (without God this is the logical conclusion and ends up with what I mentioned earlier, shame).

The way they try and protect themselves is by using their gifts (or vocation) to do the 'right' thing. They assume (again a foolish assumption) that if they do the right thing, it will offset the wrong of their being. They do right things for all the wrong reasons. They want to reduce the beauty, majesty and wonder of our Beloved into a formula for being right.

Why, there are even some in the Body there who are so foolish to think of doing the will of God as a form of being right. If you can get your honor bearer to understand this in the smallest way, consider it a major victory. If only they could see what our Beloved Jesus has accomplished for them, that they are now like us, right in their very being before our Beloved, then they would not be concerned with doing right, only expressing the right that is already in them.

Help your honor bearer to see that his need to make everything a problem is rooted in this foolishness. Help him see that his 'need' for everything to be a problem is more about his brokenness than it is about how God works. Get him to see the great dilemmas of life in the Bible.
> Faith and works.
> Three expressions, One God.

The body of Christ is full of individuals.
Different gifts, one reason to express
them.
Present reality with a glorious vision or
future.
Male and female, two in one, a
marriage.
Love your neighbor as yourself.

The list goes on. Your biggest challenge is to
get him to live in the righteousness of Jesus
that is his in full. It may take years to do this.
May you taste and experience the patience of
our Beloved amidst it all.

In the King's service,
Insight

Whisper@heaven.edu
Insight@heaven.edu
Subject: The mystery of God's vulnerability.

Dear Whisper,

It seems your honor bearer has a keen interest in studying more seriously about God. His wife is really frustrating him, and he is looking for answers. That is encouraging and comes with its own challenges for you. More on that a bit later.

I share your struggle to understand sin. It is so illogical and contrary to our way of life here but is the very fabric of their lives there. They feel the weight and burden of it daily there.

Sin causes our Beloved so much pain. But they cannot imagine an all-powerful God being vulnerable. It is inconceivable to them. They have whole books written in their philosophy (they call it theology, but it is not the study of God) with long arguments seeking to prove God cannot be vulnerable. As you know from your being here, we don't study God. We simply love Him and get to know Him through all He reveals about Himself, but never, ever in the abstract.

I often wonder why they do not consider the vulnerability of God the greatest mystery in the universe. When we see the unfaithful one and the dark world, we can only marvel at the cost our Beloved has paid. These honor bearers are so caught up in themselves that they want to figure out sin, but if they would only look a bit deeper, they could join us in worship, joyous rapturous worship. For to see the vulnerability of God on display often stops heaven in its tracks as people are so caught off guard by the space He makes for finite creation. Your honor bearer will struggle to make sense of this as it makes no sense in their world.

And yet we know, that the greatest mystery about God is that our Beloved, the single most powerful being in the universe, is also the most vulnerable being in the universe. What is a joyous mystery to us, is a terror to them.

They assume God must be the most controlling being in the universe. They confuse Sovereignty with control and end up continuing the lie of the unfaithful one that our Beloved is not good.

To say that someone has the power, wisdom and capacity to deal with anything they are confronted with is very different from saying that God is in control.

To say He is in control implies that He is either directly or indirectly causing the events. But we are back to the mystery of it again and I have no reason to continue the argument, especially here, for here we know Him as He is and are known as we are.

In the King's service,
Insight

Whisper@heaven.edu
Insight@heaven.edu
Subject: Free choice and control.

Dear Whisper,

Thank you for the honest note and sharing
your struggle with my last note. It seems you
and your honor bearer are struggling with
control and love, granted on very different
levels. Please be aware that in the dark world,
everything is a struggle. Even for us who know
the sweet air of heaven, as we enter to work in
the dark world, we can pick up the agitation of
all that is going on. Let me put in perspective
this issue of control.

Our Beloved gave the honor bearers a gift. The
simplest way to describe this gift is free choice.
God wanted a relationship with them and gave
them the capacity to choose freely to love. This
gift comes with the freedom to defend
themselves and the responsibility to protect
what is assigned to them.

If we go back to the Garden of Eden, we see the
unfaithful one trying to seduce Eve. He is lying to
her and calling God selfish. He is attacking the
character of our Beloved. He is trying to
corrupt the image of God she was to carry in
her heart. We already talked about this, but the
point here is that she was responsible to guard,
watch over and defend her heart. The gift of
free will comes with the gift to defend. Eve
should have defended herself, all she needed

to do was say, 'NO' to the unfaithful one and the argument was over.

As we all know through innumerable tears, she didn't say no. She opened a door by her choice that left humanity in deep trouble. They now have a gift to protect but with nothing to defend. They have the gift to guard but have nothing to watch over. To say this is confusing for them is an understatement.

So, they turn the gift and try and protect themselves and that is now a part of the very challenge before them. They use the gift to protect themselves from anything that threatens them. And as we know, God is the most 'threatening' being in the universe, that is if you are a rebel. (I admit I am terrified of Him at times, especially when He shows up and I have not had the time to prepare myself for the overwhelming glory that comes with Him. But that will make absolutely no sense to these dear little ones so don't even bother trying to explain it. All they will hear you say is that you are afraid of Him, which could not be further from the truth.)

It doesn't surprise me to hear you describe your honor bearer as a control freak. In truth, they all are, at a heart level. You are right in seeing it most clearly in his relationship with his wife and with his students as well. Those closest to him, those he cares most about, will often be the hardest ones for him to be vulnerable with. The simplest way to help him deal with control issues in these important relationships is to teach him the discipline of getting his 'agenda' or purpose for dealing with the issue out in the open as soon as possible in the relationship. This simple act in these key relationships will help him slow down and walk more authentically, with transparency, in these relationships.

Broken honor bearers are consumed with a "need" to control life. Every moment is spent trying to get as much power as possible so they might control everything within reach. Being vulnerable is sheer terror to them. So, they project onto God their anxiety and assume He is a control freak too. Misuse of the free choice gift and a distorted perception of God cause them to defend themselves from an illusionary God they created out of their broken heart.

Your honor bearer will struggle with control, which is often translated in their thinking and longing for certainty. They long for physical certainty because they feel so unsafe in their brokenness. God doesn't promise them physical certainty, He promises them relational certainty, which is what they are really longing for, but they often don't know it.

They need to change their focus to that of self-control, which really is the challenge before them and the opportunity they are offered by the Spirit of our Beloved. That task alone will keep any human wrestling with discipline for a good portion of their life.

In the King's service,
Insight

Whisper@heaven.edu
Insight@heaven.edu
Subject: His will

Dear Whisper,

It seems your honor bearer has a continuing
interest in studying the Bible. This may sound
a bit surprising, but there are some concerns
you should be aware of if and when your
honor bearer looks at this from an academic
discipline mindset. Their systems for trying to
understand God are often their own finite
ideas for putting God in a box.

Most who study God academically end up so
in their head, they lose their love for Him. As I
wrote earlier, their preoccupation with control,
certainty and making everything a problem to
be solved has great influence over their study.
They use knowledge as a source of power to
get certainty. They make God a problem to be
solved so they can be right. They end up with
an abstract argument with no heart involved or
vulnerability in a relationship.

Our Beloved doesn't want to be studied, He
wants to love them and be loved. Help your
honor bearer see that knowledge without
relationship is worthless.

You also mentioned that your honor bearer is
struggling with the 'will of God'. This takes us
back to the human assumption that God is
controlling. I am sure if you probed deep

enough, you would discover his idea of heaven is the place where life is dictated by God in every detail. "Turn left here, now turn right, now eat this fruit, but only at this time…" I must confess it brings a smile to my face at the absurdity of it.

You might remind your honor bearer to think of being a father and the future of raising kids. Help him see that even in all his brokenness, the directions he gives a young child are for their safety or development. 'Don't touch this hot stove. Eat this food. Don't say those words…" But as the child grows up, the honor bearer gives him or her more space to make their decisions and own their choices. A good father's primary concern is that he will respect and love the family and live out the values vital to holding them together. Get him to see the humor (or pain) of a father telling their 21-year-old son or daughter how to live every detail of their life. An earthly honor bearer longs for his children to grow into loving, responsible adults. He doesn't want to micromanage them. He wants to free them. In the same sense -- only magnify it a billion percent -- God longs to give them freedom. He doesn't want to micromanage them. They must grow up.

Please bear with me as I know it may take years for your honor bearer to grasp this. Remember what God is trying to do and then help him take baby steps towards freedom.

In the King's service,
Insight

Whisper@heaven.edu
Insight@heaven.edu
Subject: The in-between space

Dear Whisper,

I thought I had prepared you for what you would be facing down there, but when I read these words from your last message it was shockingly clear that more instruction is needed:

> This world is darker than I imagined. Is it possible that I am on the very edge of Hell? Surely there is no place worse than this!
>
> There are educational systems that can't teach. There are governments that can't govern; churches that won't reveal truth and grace; businesses that don't exchange goods and services; technologies that hurt rather than help the quality of life; arts that celebrate sin and darkness; and families that don't understand unconditional love and acceptance.

Sadly, your description of the in-between place is accurate. For those who have refused the love of our Father, it will only get worse for all eternity. For those who have turned back to Our Beloved Father, they will see their world as the start of Heaven, and it will only get better into all eternity. Our Beloved doesn't just want to live in them, He wants them to take a part in His Kingdom.

Your description sets forth the challenges His Kingdom people face in trying to build a container that will hold the effects of a Visitation. Right now, these institutions are so fragmented that any revealed Presence will quickly slip through the gaps.

All of us working down there are shocked the first time we realize how many humans think The Author of all life is only interested in the spiritual world. What they call the church.

I have so much more to say to you about their systems and how you might get your honor bearer to work in them. I will write of this later.

In the King's service,
Insight

Whisper@heaven.edu
Insight@heaven.edu
Subject: Humility 1

Dear Whisper,

Thank you for your service. Thank you for taking the wisdom of our Beloved and working so diligently to help these creatures of dust. I so enjoy reading your notes and how you explain your growing love for God and His ways amidst the dark world. Once again, we understand God uses all things to reveal Himself. One of the hardest things for honor bearers like yours to understand is the humility of our Beloved. In their dark world the continual struggle for power causes them to assume that God has no need to be humble. They see humility as a sign of weakness instead of greatness.

I know you are aware of these things, but please bear with me as I go back to the basics on reality here in The City of God. I am also aware that because of the darkness there, these basics are forgotten or harder to see in the fog of arrogance.

This morning I went for a walk in the garden, and I felt so encouraged and restored after seeing the beauty and wisdom of our Beloved on display. He loves to create flowers. Then He entrusts their care to His gardeners who create new colors and expressions with each new season. I found an orchid this morning that was gold, traces of yellow and red. It was stunning, and I had a clear sense of the pleasure of God in what they are doing. They named it 'sunset', because of its colors. Anyway, it got me thinking about humility and what we have been talking about recently. Of course, it takes me back to the SHOCKING moment when Jesus was sent to the dark world.

Our Beloved called the whole City together to reveal His plans for the honor bearers. Our Beloved announced that Jesus was going to do down among the honor bearers. We thought, surely He was going to put on a display of His great power for all the dark world to see and fear. Then, Jesus came forward and stood before us. He gave His scepter to His Father. Then He slowly lifted the crown of light off His head and set it in His Father's hand. Slowly, ever so slowly, His glowing glorious power and presence was diminishing. The whole City stood in awe and had no idea what was going on. We stared at Him and The Father, back and forth, as the 'gap' between them became wider and wider.

Then, in a moment, He was gone. His presence was missing among us for the first time, ever. We felt an ache and realized we had taken His presence for granted all our lives. The Father also ached. He was staring at the dark planet, and in that moment, we realized Jesus had become a baby in a woman's uterus. I weep as I write this as you cannot imagine in that dark place the choice He made to humble Himself.

In one instant, He is among us as light and wisdom, holding the very structure of the universe together and the next moment, He has given it all up, He has emptied Himself of all the privileges of God and has taken on the role of God in the finite presence of a dust body.

Then the Father spoke to us and said He was going to reveal the very substance of His heart to the universe. We were invited to watch it and learn all we could from it.

I can only say, it left us stunned. There was a silence over The City that in a strange way, we would get used to over the next 33 Earth years. His life in the dark world, His interactions, His words, every moment of every day were talked about in a reverence and as a form of worship that has never been felt before.

That was the day I realized the joy of eternity. We had all assumed we knew God. We enjoyed and celebrated His presence. But in that moment, we realized there was a wisdom, a profound and infinite depth to Him, riches beyond our wildest imagination, an unending storehouse of treasures that He could reveal to us. We could look forward to deeper and richer revelations of who He was for all eternity because He was eternal. As this revelation washed over me, I have never been the same. I have a hope and joy for Earth, and The City will never be the same again.

I cannot express the joy it is to serve Him. I know you know this but remember Who we are working for and it is only then that everything takes on a life-giving perspective and encouragement to keep going in our own humility.

In the King's service,
Insight

Whisper@heaven.edu
Insight@heaven.edu
Subject: A side note

Dear Whisper,

I thought you might enjoy a simple story of the joy that awaits you when you return here. Last night we had a long meal with friends. A close friend was talking about an invention he was working on for years. He said it all started with a simple question, "Is light a wave or a particle?" He knew it was a question placed in his heart by our Creator.

The reason I say this is because as we talked about it long into the evening, we realized that each of us had walked into a new discovery, relationship or invention in the same way, it all began with a question in our heart placed there by our Beloved. We discovered our Beloved was asking all of us questions that sent us on a joyous journey to explore and discover what He did and how something works with the purpose of creating something new that serves and honor each other and our relationships.

Oh, the splendor, joy and beauty of an infinite Being who is more interested in asking us questions and getting us involved in our world than just dictating to us His will as if a cloned behavior is all that matters.

I was wondering, what questions are tugging at your heart? You don't need to reply, I just wanted you to slow down and recognize there

will be questions growing from your work
with your honor bearer and your involvement
in that dark place that might grow into years of
research and a new creative expression of our
Beloved.

In the King's service,
Insight

Whisper@heaven.edu
Insight@heaven.edu
Subject: Humility 2

Dear Whisper,

I am glad you were able to use advice from an earlier note. Your honor bearer's accident, and the person hurt because of it, offers a perfect chance to help him understand humility as we talked about it. His intense feelings of responsibility and shame are exactly what the unfaithful one would use against him to try to destroy your work. They so quickly assume that anything that goes wrong is their fault and then shame enters and creates more darkness. Being finite means they will make mistakes and that mistakes are normal for creatures of dust. Mistakes are not sin, they just happen in a dark and broken world. I am so glad you helped him get a peek at shame and then talk about it with his friend. Well done.

If your honor bearer was in an accident that he was responsible for, the natural response would be for him to humble himself and take responsibility for it. But we're trying to teach him even deeper things about humility. The dust people have such a distorted picture of our Beloved. Sin has created a brokenness in them that makes it hard for them to understand the depth of His love and humility. Of course, you see the effects of their brokenness all around you. Sin has affected every relationship they have.

The idea that One who is pure and holy would take on all the sin of the dark world still baffles people like your honor bearer. I admit that it astounds me too. How can God be so humble in this way? There is not a grain of darkness in our Beloved. Yet He emptied Himself and took on the nature of humanity. He became one of them.

And then THE MOMENT came. With weeping I write of that horrible/glorious time when THE ONE allowed the creatures He breathed into existence, to nail HIM to a cross, to kill HIM, to put HIM to death. He took on Himself their brokenness. Such an act of Humility is beyond words to us here. Never, in a million billion years would it have entered our mind, the depth of who He truly was and is and is to be. We all knew He was good, righteous, faithful, kind, merciful and gracious. These we knew about Him as trees know the sun. But when we saw His love for these honor bearers, when we saw it, experienced it, with Him on the cross, we realized in THE MOMENT that our Beloved was Infinitely beautiful in every aspect of His character.

I know your honor bearer wears a cross as a religious symbol, but we can barely even look at one without being overwhelmed with awe. When we meet with The ONE here in The City, we never see a hint of the agony he endured on that Cross. He exudes joy in everything He does. He invites us past this shyness we feel about it and laughs with us in sheer joy at what it revealed about The Beloved. To be honest, it will take us thousands of years to grow into that revelation, but oh the joy ahead of us. If you can plant a seed of this joy in your honor bearer, if you can put the smallest splinter of light into his spirit, it will give him hope and a future joy that is unspeakable and truly worth looking forward to.

I know this is no small challenge for you there in the dark place, but please know you have the support of all who are here to help you in any way we can. Please feel free to ask of anything that you might need from us.

In the King's service,
Insight

Whisper@heaven.edu
Insight@heaven.edu
Subject: Humility 3

Dear Whisper,

I sympathize with your struggle. You must not
compare what we know with what they can
know. Because of the currents of evil there,
dwellers in the dark world will struggle their
whole life. That is why THE ONE said if their
faith is as small as a mustard seed, they could
move mountains. It is not about the amount of
faith they have, it is about living in the faith
they have. I heard one of our wise ones say
that it is like a bubble that is compressed at the
depths of the ocean. Because of the pressure, it
is small and seems insignificant. But as the
bubble rises to the surface it grows larger and
larger because it is given freedom to expand.
So, a small amount of faith on earth, when
given the freedom of Heaven, will
exponentially expand in wonderful ways.

One thing we haven't discussed is the 3rd
strand of humility, concerning their individual
uniqueness and abilities. Our Beloved went to
great lengths to give each honor bearer distinct
finger prints, voice prints, DNA, etc. That is
just in the physical sense. In the spiritual sense,
they have gifts, strengths and unique
perspectives through their personality, family
and culture. Each of these gifts is an expression
of God in them. To walk in, express and reveal
their gifts is the fullness of humility in them. To

walk in humility is to express their gift, in faith, in a way that honors who God is in you.

Now back to the purpose of these notes, our Beloved is the humblest being in the universe. He is the source, foundation and essence of all gifts. All good things are found in Him. He gives gifts to each honor bearer and therefore, each expression can only truly be seen in light of who He is.

For our Beloved to humble Himself, it is simply to make clear that all life (gifts, strengths, capacities) are rooted in Him. Imagine if you would, a garden. If you took what the soil gave to plants, what the sun gave to plants, what water and seasons gave to plants and put all those ingredients together in what they offered, then you might begin to understand what God is to all of life.

The humblest thing God can do, is to be God. If He was not God and was acting like it, it would be arrogance. If He is God and is not acting like it, it would be arrogance. If you are the source of all things, then you must act, live and relate to people as if you are.

Now I embarrass myself as I speak of things that are so elementary. They are the air we breathe. Just as a fish does not even think about water until they are out of it. So, you will realize much of how we live and move here is not even questioned until you get to the dark planet. As you mentioned in the last note, it is shocking what they question and do not know.

Do not be shocked, that is the fruit of darkness and deception. Just as with cancer when discovered in them, it will make them question the meaning of life, so darkness will require them to rethink the most basic elements of our Beloved and His creation.

I marvel at our Beloved's willingness to start over with them. There is no limit to His humility in starting where they are and then working with them to grow towards all He purposes for them.

In summary, you can't easily separate out the three aspects of humility. Each of the expressions of humility are woven together in their dark world, and it takes time and discipline to learn how to work with each area. They will embrace that they are finite and therefore, each gift they use is limited and needs to grow and be developed. They are broken and will be severely tempted to hide in their gift to protect their brokenness. Yet if they don't deal with their brokenness, they will fear weakness and vulnerability which further separates them from the wisdom of our Beloved.

In the King's service,
Insight

Whisper@heaven.edu
Insight@heaven.edu
Subject: Issues of the heart.

Dear Whisper,

I know you are being kind and not wanting to
burden me with the challenges you face. I
sensed in the last note that you are struggling
with getting your honor bearer to be aware of
things going on in his heart. He attends a
church, gives money and even reads his Bible,
but I sense you are anxious about him not
dealing with issues of the heart. You are
perceptive to see that he is 'hiding' in his job.
Meaning more and more of his value and
identity is clinging to his work and he now
uses it as a way to 'protect' himself, justify
himself and just simply as a way to avoid
talking to our Beloved about the pains of life. I
know his relationship with his wife is also
stressed and not doing well.

The heart, the center of their being, the core of
their choices, is the gift of God to us all. All free
beings have been given this space, which is
ours, with only one law, written into our very
DNA to govern and guide it.

The law is simply this, 'Give to each aspect of
creation what it is worth', or another way of
saying it is, "Let an object or being's worth
define your relationship to it." This simple law,
that true value rules our life, is as natural as
breathing here in The City. Respect is simply
the fruit of what has clear value. We naturally

interact with this respect because we have a clear source of value that defines all of us, our relationships and all interactions with this created world, beginning in The City.

Now I will state the most obvious fact to us, God is the most valuable being in the universe. Words cannot describe the joy, celebration and sheer ecstasy of being near HIM. When our Beloved, our Leader or our Wisdom comes near us, everything around us becomes more genuine; tastes, smells, sights and sounds become more intense, tangible or penetrating. He is very sensitive not to overwhelm us for we could easily 'explode' at the sheer revelation of it all.

When all this is happening, our heart tingles or vibrates with the awareness of this BEING, He is holding all reality together. That all life is in HIM, through HIM and is being pulled to HIM. This is accompanied by a growing revelation of HIS value, worth and significance. It is at this moment that ultimate reality becomes crystal clear to us. We know He is WORTHY.

No one knows time in this place of being. It is as if it stops when we are in His presence. Some have 'woken' up and days have passed, and they had no sense of time passing at all. Our Beloved assures us it is normal to "miss Him" when we awaken. It is just difficult to go back to the 'world' around us after having 'touched' Him.

Your honor bearer was made for this deep connection. It is what he desires in the very essence of his being and doesn't even know it. Because of sin no human being can experience this anymore.

When the great rebellion took place and Adam and Eve broke from the family of God, they hid, not from God, but from themselves. They could not bear the thought of being close to Him, of feeling this overwhelming revelation of His worthiness and knowing they had chosen to listen to a creature who had so little value compared to our Beloved. They had missed the mark, chosen to listen to the unfaithful one, and rebelled from, 'He who is Worthy', and were separated from Him because of it. This experience now defines them, and the truly sad part is that most of them don't even know it anymore.

When we talked about brokenness earlier and it being a part of humility, this is the core issue of it at a heart level. They know He is worthy, and they have nothing to give Him, no way to respond. They are banished from His presence and that is the most painful place in the universe to be.

In the King's service,
Insight

Insight@heaven.edu
Whisper@heaven.edu
Subject: Correcting his value system

Dear Whisper,

Now, in light of the last email and our reality here, we must slow down and help your honor bearer work his way back to understanding and working with his own heart. It will be like a foreign object to him that you must help him learn to understand and work with.

Remember, where your honor bearer's treasure is, that is where his heart will be. So, our work is to help him see and revel in the value (treasure) of God. He doesn't know it yet, but his own value ranks highest for what is valuable to him. They might call it self-interest, but it is nothing more than selfishness.

Now it is important here to differentiate between having a healthy value and selfishness. In group-centered cultures, any self-valuing is called selfishness and causes much confusion among them. The group cultures assume the individual has no value outside of the group. This is a form of slavery and not in the heart of God. In an individual-centered culture, they define themselves and their value as independence from all others. This is also a form of slavery, only to their desires, rather than the group.

Until they get a true picture of our Beloved, they will never truly know their own value.

They are made in His image. Only as they sense His great worth and their sense of being image bearers will they begin to truly see how valuable they are to Him. Of course, He is the only One who can state something's value, but they don't believe that in their dark world.

One aspect of being made in His image is that their heart is creative. Our Beloved creates out of nothing. That is what makes Him so spectacular, He draws from the power of His own being and creates. The honor bearer's creative ability is not to create out of nothing, but to take what God has given to him and create with it.

What this translates into for them is that they give meaning to what God has created in their world. They are meaning makers. They can take anything that our Beloved has created and give meaning to it. They can also rename it and give a different meaning to it.

They rarely realize the power of this gift. They have the delegated authority to define their own perspective and not even our Beloved will force them to change it. I think you will see this most clearly in their struggle to name the cells in a woman's uterus. Do they call it a child or just a growth? How they name it will define the meaning they give to it and how they relate to it.

We cannot conceive of such a struggle. That they can rename 'life' without consequences is beyond us, that is for sure. The very reason we call it a dark world is because they have named their world, life and their relationships contrary to the very purposes of our Beloved.

They have renamed creation / to evolution.
They have renamed love / to sex.
They have renamed church / as a building.
They have renamed your spouse / to your partner.
They have renamed sin / as sickness.
They have named identity / as gender.
They have renamed freedom / as having no responsibility.
They have named power / the source of life.
They have named control / the purpose of life.
They have named independence / the goal of life.

Darkness is not the absence of meaning (that is madness), but it is the changing of meaning from the purposes of God. Don't even try to understand the variety of names they give to life. It will only confuse you more. Just keep your eyes on Wisdom and she will guide you to help your honor bearer work out this in his life.

In the next note, I will try and give you some examples of how to do this.

In the King's service,
Insight

Insight@heaven.edu
Whisper@heaven.edu
Subject: Source of evil

Dear Whisper,

I notice you are silent. Here in The City we take silence as a gift. Our Beloved uses silence as a form of communication. He never withholds communication and withdraws from us. That only happens in the dark world. People there fear silence because in quietness they are confronted with their heart. Therefore, they avoid it as they might avoid a sickness. They also use it as a form of punishment in the sense that if someone is upset at you, they will not speak to you as a form of punishment. I can say with great joy that it never happens here. Silence gives space for another person to express their heart. We know we are at a special place in our relationships when we can sit and be silent with each other.

This takes me back to the issues of the heart. I trust you don't assume you can analyze your honor bearer's heart and thus understand it like you would any other object. There is a mystery to it and it will always remain such to us. Again, that is what makes relationships a mystery, they are created and maintained by a mysterious heart.

Remember again what happened in the Garden. Did you know it was the size of several states down where you are? Well, Adam and Eve had no idea of the power of their heart and no real perception of evil. Today the honor bearers can see clearly, painfully clearly, the fruit of their choices. They can see the evil around them, but they are militantly ignorant of their hearts being a source of evil. That single idea will be the hardest ground to break open so that the kingdom of God can take root there.

Your work is to slowly help your honor bearer to "own" his heart. That's always the starting place. Once he owns the evil and brokenness there, he will be set free. All of us know it is now a dark world and there is evil in all the systems. But the starting place is always in their own heart. That is where the real 'battle' is being fought. Our Beloved will not hold them responsible for the ripple effects of their sin, the SAVIOR has taken care of that. He has offered them a new heart, but they must learn to walk into it. They must take the heart replacement and learn to live it out and grow into it. That is what our Beloved calls maturity.

I must confess it has taken us years to understand what our Beloved is doing. It was a complete mystery to us, we held the tension of it knowing that He was up to something and we had no idea what it was.

We now anticipate each person coming and walking through the gates here. Angels often line up to see the most incredible transformation of earthly faith into a Heavenly faith. I have no words to describe what a weak and struggling honor bearer is on earth and when they walk into the pure air of His presence here, in a matter of moments, they morph into powerful beings that will rule and reign with our Beloved. It will be our joy to serve them as well.

Build faith in your honor bearer, know this, what seems small and insignificant there, will be the basis of supernatural presence here as soon as they walk through the gates to enter The City. Let that hope, that anticipation, be a part of the joy you have there, it will sustain you through many long hours in darkness.

In the King's service,
Insight

Insight@heaven.edu
Whisper@heaven.edu
Subject: Naming and tracking emotions.

Dear Whisper,

In talking so much about the heart, I don't want to neglect your well-expressed concerns about the honor bearer's emotions. The values of the human heart communicate through their emotions. The values are not always rational for that is the way their minds work. But they can always be understood and expressed in feelings. You can think of it as emotions are the fruit of the values. As there has been so much pain in their world, most of them have shut down their emotions to protect themselves. As a result, they have no language to explain or even engage their emotions.

They got it backwards, their primary mode of functioning is not rational with feelings as optional or in the background, but they are made to feel (value) with the added capacity to think. The mind was meant to serve the heart. Do not let this be an 'either / or', 'this or that' problem to be solved, as both are required. The honor bearers love to swing back and forth as if one could exist without the other. They were meant to lead with the heart and then the head gives them the capacity to understand it, put language to it and build a relationship as a result.

So, help your honor bearer get to know his heart by teaching him to become aware of his feelings and to name them. Is he disappointed? Frustrated? Sad? Grieving? Furious? Each word describes a certain tempo, intensity, time frame and should produce a desired outcome. It seems clear that your honor bearer is distant from his wife. He has shut down some aspects of his emotions to protect himself. Work with him to specifically name those feelings.

Once he has clearly named an emotion, help him to follow it to the source. Just like a fire puts out smoke and if you want to find the fire, follow the smoke. So, remember, values express themselves with emotions. Whatever emotions he expresses can be tracked to the source, his values. Only then can you understand and work with the heart. Work at naming the emotions and thus values he received as a child. Help him clarify his relationship to his mother and clarify his fear of disappointing her.

Even as I put that in writing, it has a measured analysis that we can stand back from and gain insight on but sounds a bit like it is all in the mind. Emotions are messy. Here, we enjoy the surprise that emotions bring us, we look forward to them and how they will color and add depth to the relationships we are enjoying. But where you are, emotions rage like spurting volcanoes as their flesh tries to use them for its own sadistic pleasures and false comforts.

A part of your work is to get the honor bearer to see salvation as more than a one-time event. He needs a growing dependence on the Wisdom and Power of our Father and to be able to name his emotions and bring them all to our Beloved.

In the King's service,
Insight

Insight@heaven.edu
Whisper@heaven.edu
Subject: Sharing pain.

Dear Whisper,

I ache with you as you described the pain of the miscarriage for your honor bearer and his beautiful wife. I know you were almost as excited as they were and now you experience the pain of the loss of this dear little one. I know it feels overwhelming and you are struggling in how to help them deal with the pain of it.

Let me tie the last email I wrote into this as I realize that in the last note I talked mostly about the honor bearers and didn't give you an appropriate context for why these emotions are so vital. I made some assumptions. I apologize for perhaps implying that these painful emotions are only about them. They are not. As this might seem a bit harsh to say at this point in their pain, let me stand back and look at this from the heart of our Beloved.

We have and celebrate emotions because our Beloved has them. He has strong emotions and is passionate about some things and angry about others. I mentioned earlier about the mystery of vulnerability, this is a key piece of it.

I know your honor bearer will have a hard time believing it but Wisdom weeps and can be deeply grieved. That our Beloved is afflicted and aches with the pain the honor bearers are going through. I can't put into words the sight of the Almighty Sovereign Lord of the Universe weeping over the pains humanity struggles with.

It does not happen often, but when I AM weeps, it is as if time stops. The City feels it and walks quieter, talks softer and listens more intently. To see it with your own eyes, is the wonder of the universe. Our Beloved is so pure that you know the tears are the exact expression of His own heart. I must say, when I saw it, I was undone. I would have done anything, anything to help Him, but he touched my own heart and told me not to fear the pain but to embrace it as a new part of our relationship.

That thought would have never entered my mind, but once I did that, once I turned the pain into something shared between us, I realized, Oh the Glory, the unspeakable Grandeur, Splendor and Majesty of our Beloved to share that with us. We would have never known He loved so deeply, but now we do. We have shared something so intimate, so personal, so real, that it has changed me forever.

Now, back to the pain of your honor bearer and his wife. They are experiencing deep loss and pain as a result of the miscarriage. Help them to see that our Beloved longs to 'share' that pain with them. That through it a deeper intimacy can be birthed and even in such deep pain, a beauty can come out of it in their relationship with Him.

There is a lot of pain in their dark work, but when I realized the intimacy that can come out of it, I am in awe of His willingness to humble Himself to meet them in the midst of that pain. Oh, the comfort of our Beloved is beyond words and heals the deepest suffering.

The fact that The Almighty feels so strongly is the foundation for honor bearers owning their own feelings and sharing them with our Beloved. If they world take the risk and hear His pain and then share their pain with Him, they would be transformed by the comfort and thus intimacy of it.

In the King's service,
Insight

Subject: What determines value?

Dear Whisper,

Your interest in better understanding values and the importance they play is good. I appreciate the questions as it helps me to know where you are and what you understand and don't understand. Values are the foundation upon all clear thinking there. Let me review why it is so important, so your work is more effective.

The ability to understand something's value is the basis for freedom and choice. Value and choice are like a lock and key. You can't understand the one without the other.

Take a couple of coins that the image bearers use. If one is a penny and the other a twenty-five-cent piece. Which would they choose? They don't even have to think about it. Once they perceive that one coin has a greater value, they choose the larger value. Now, what if it was a rare and valuable penny? That would make it more valuable than the quarter. That information would influence their decision, but they still make the choice based on their perception of value.

The comparison of a penny and a quarter is absurd if seen from our side. Our Beloved makes streets of The City out of gold and its gates out of a single Pearl. But I am sure this description of The City is only making you homesick and that will not do.

Obviously, you want to influence the honor bearer's values. In essence, his decision-making process is a clarifying process of understanding something's value. To help you think clearly, here are some characteristics that determine something's value.

Uniqueness
The more unique something is the more value it has. The harder it is to find the more energy is spent on obtaining it; the less there is for whoever wants it, the more the image bearers are willing to pay to get it.

Beauty
The more beautiful something is, the more value it has. Although different people will have different ideas about what is beautiful, all things made by our Beloved Father have an element of beauty in them.

Quality, purity and durability
The quality of what you are choosing also determines value. How pure is it? Who long will it last? The purer, higher quality something has in it, the more value it has.

Need / Want
Their need versus their want of something. If you gave your honor bearer a choice between air to breathe and millions of pieces of the paper they call currency, which would he take?

He would take the air because he needs it to survive in his world.

Now let me tie it all together. What is the most unique, beautiful, long-lasting and needed thing in the universe? It is the glory of God's being. It holds together all things in the whole universe. He is IT, there is no other. Why this is important is that to choose His nature as our defining reference point is the most humble thing He can do.

I have given you enough to think about and to wrestle with for a while. Let me know where you think the honor bearers have problems with it.

In the King's service,
Insight

Whisper@heaven.edu
Insight@heaven.edu
Subject: Value is the foundation for love

Dear Whisper,

I am slow to respond to your last email as it really got me thinking. You mentioned that your honor bearer is struggling with loving his wife and later you write about how every song or story there is about love. Your question, straight from the mouth of a singer there, 'What's love got to do with it?' stirred me to the depths of my soul.

I guess I have forgotten more than I realized in regard to The City and the dark world. I assumed I remembered life there and was talking about love clearly in the last email, but it seems I have forgotten the struggle of working in a dark world where the meaning of words are quickly lost.

Thank you for pushing back and asking about love, for it is the thread that holds all of these emails together. I forgot how The City has a way of clarifying our thinking, perception and awareness the moment you start to breathe the air here.

When I email about values and how worthy our Beloved is, I assumed you could see clearly that I was talking about love. Values are the foundation of love, or you could say in order to love something, you must know its value.

Once the question of 'what is something worth' is answered, then and only then do you have a foundation to love it appropriately. The very reason their world is defined as 'darkness' is because they have lost any basis of value for their choices. As one of their writers said, 'They know the cost of everything but the value of nothing.'

The whole basis of moral obligation is rooted in value. Another way of saying it is that the whole reason you are supposed to choose one thing over another is because of its greater value. This reality is seen clearest in our Beloved. The reason they are required to love Him above anything else, to choose him over themselves, is because He is the most valuable being in the universe.

It is the language of the heart. For the simple reality is that what they truly treasure, that is where their heart is. When our Beloved writes to them to watch over their heart, what He is saying is that they must watch over the things their heart treasures.

In regard to his struggling to love his wife, the fundamental question is, can he value her when she is struggling or imperfect? He will need the Father's love for this. Of course, it will start within himself with the same question. Can he value himself when he is struggling or imperfect? Once he knows the love of the Father for himself, it will be much easier to love his wife with that love.

Let me know if you have any questions or if there is any lack of clarity as this foundation is vital for any sense of understanding our Beloved or the very foundation of The City.

In the King's service,
Insight

Whisper@heaven.edu
Insight@heaven.edu
Subject: How does discipleship work?

Dear Whisper,

You wrote in your last email, 'Why don't you
tell me what to do with my honor bearer? You
give a hint of direction and that is all.' That is a
good question we all struggle with at times.
When I committed to helping you, it was not to
dictate directions but to help you gently lead
the honor bearer toward a deeper relationship
through this. That's how we work, even
between us, that's why we communicate often
and why I am walking with you through this.
One of the best helps you can give is to get him
into relationship with others who are
struggling to love God. Help connect them at a
heart level.

Our Beloved always works through
relationships. Help your honor bearer find a
small group of people he can share his life
with. You can guide him, but our Beloved
keeps the awareness of our presence to a
minimum so that they don't become mystics
and get distracted by us.

Whisper, let me be clear. Our Beloved wants a
partnership, a deep and personal relationship
with the honor bearers. He has no intention of
controlling them and wants each of them to
discover and walk in the grace He has offered
them. They must learn to own the new life He
has given them. The only way they can do this

is by taking the risk to show up and have continuing relationship with Him. The ways of our Beloved in The City are always rooted in the "risk of expressing our love for Him through our choices in this relationship."

His purpose for these honor bearers is very different from any other aspect of creation. He has purposed from the very beginning that they would be leaders, rulers and guardians of the earth. They are invited into a realm of power and leadership we angels have never seen.

They sell themselves so short and assume they are nothing, a grain in the sands of time. They think so little of themselves that they can't imagine greatness and have lost the plot of our Beloved for them.

Now back to your question about offering 'help' to you. You also must learn the ways of our Beloved in leadership development. If I told you everything to do, if I laid out a prescription and gave you the 'menu' of how we work, then the most natural progression would be for you to do that with your honor bearer.

I know you feel the pressure as you hear his prayers to help him "get it right." You feel the sense of his own urgency as he wants to be told all that he is to do so that he is safe. This is so that he won't have to bear the weight of his own choices.

The blessed joy of The City is that each being here is perfectly free. There is no control needed here in any aspect of life. We work from the heart and adore our Father. It is the purest air we breathe here and there is no fear.

In the King's service,
Insight

Whisper@heaven.edu
Insight@heaven.edu
Subject: Risk and being fully present.

Dear Whisper,

It is interesting how words can take on such different meanings. In The City, we are aware of risk in our relationships, but our risk is not rooted in nor has it any part in fear. We are not afraid of sin, that is never a part of our thinking. We might make mistakes (forget a name, drop something, trip or lose something… your honor bearer will have this idea of perfection that means we never make a mistake, but that honor is only for our Beloved), but they are only 'allowed' so that we might experience the joy of growth through them. We cannot stretch beyond our boundaries without taking a risk. Any growth requires some level of risk. However, failure is not feared here, it is our purest pleasure to see our limitations and learn through our mistakes in that it creates a deeper relationship with others. If you hinted at this with your honor bearer, he would struggle as he cannot conceive of anything related to heaven with mistakes.

I trust you notice that we are back to the first thread of humility. That we are limited, finite and it is our joy. Of course, they cannot imagine this, but they can begin to grow into it as they discover the grace of our Beloved.

Risk is what limited, finite creation is always confronted with. You mentioned in your response that your honor bearer is finding the relationship with his boss very difficult. In the words I am talking about here, he is having a hard time being honest with his boss about issues going on inside of him. He has lost his voice and gone silent. He is afraid that if he 'shows up' he will be rejected and find himself alone. He has taken the safe route and refuses to be honest and humble enough to express what he really thinks and feels. What your honor bearer really fears is not risk, but what might be revealed about him through the risk.

Here is a primary difference between The City of Light and their planet of darkness. It is our greatest joy to be fully present. To show up, to reveal all that is in us through our choice. Yes, we might play games and have fun in getting people to guess what is going on inside of us, but never, ever would we consider hiding a part of our heart from another for the primary reason that we didn't want to be known for who or what we are.

With each decision made or experience in life, we become different and our inner world takes on a new color, sound or uniqueness through it. That is why it is not stale here, for I can already hear you say if you are fully known, what is the fun of that. But you are only known in the past tense, if a moment has passed, you have already grown, developed and changed. God gave each of us a unique body so that we might understand how our spirit is on a far greater scale. The closer you get to our Beloved, the more unique you become. To spend time in His presence, even for just one pure moment, changes you. No wait, it doesn't change you, it is a bit like a kaleidoscope, one small twist and it changes because you moved it. In a far richer way, our Beloved is so infinitely creative, that to allow Him to touch you with His presence, and you become more you in a distinctive way. That will not make sense in your dark world, for light is to be feared, but here, all the full colors of light are released in new ways through HIM.

In the dark planet, their whole life is spent in hiding. From the very first moment in the Garden, Adam and Eve's first response was to hide and protect themselves. As we watched, we naively thought they would go running to our Beloved and seek His forgiveness, but to see the fruit of darkness so immediately in their life, to hide their presence from the presence of our Beloved was shocking to say the least.

Now, your hardest, most challenging, and possibly also your most rewarding work, is to teach your honor bearer to learn how to be present as a light in the dark world. They are so used to hiding, putting on a mask or just pretending to be something else on the outside that it rarely enters their thinking that when the heart is not connected to their choice to be present, they are moving further into the dark.

We have costume parties here as expressions of joy and celebration. We put on a mask or costume in order to show new parts of ourselves or a new awareness of our Beloved as seen through creation, relationships or just revelation. We love the mystery of it, but there is no hiding in it.

Faith is only truly seen in their choice to be present. It is slow, tedious work to say the least. Your honor bearer would rather hide in the law or a church or even his family or job, but beware, Wisdom is always found in being fully present in the moment.

In the King's service,
Insight

Whisper@heaven.edu
Insight@heaven.edu
Subject: Sexuality

Dear Whisper,

You ask, "Can sexuality be a mask or a place to hide?" You mention your honor bearers struggle to work with some of the kids who are confused in their gender. You are starting to understand how darkness distorts everything there. When darkness works its way into the core of their being, it leads to complete loss of identity.

That's a terrifying thing for them. Identity was meant to be a compass. Just as the needle points in a direction and gives a reference point, so their identity was given as a reference point for reality.

Now, going back to your question about sexuality and identity. Their flesh loves the instant gratification of sex. In order to intensify this, they build up a glorified image of sexuality. In a culture where there is little food, added weight becomes that standard of beauty. In a culture of abundance, skinny becomes the standard of beauty. They have accepted the false idea that beauty or sexuality defines their very identity and is their greatest source of pleasure.

As you only just entered the dark world, you will be confused by all this. The reason they are struggling so much with sexuality is because they have given up their identity to it. Anything they set up to define themselves will eventually create an identity crisis as it cannot hold the weight of their own definition. For example, there is now talk of 'transgender' and even 'nongender'. Some of them realize they cannot be defined by their sexuality and don't know what to do as a result of it. They are refusing to go deep enough to see it is not about sexuality at all.

Our Beloved made it so easy for them in the beginning. Their gender was a male and a female. The female came from the male to give them a sense of their being in this together. However, rather than having a deeper common identity in God, they became shallow to the point that their anatomy defined them. Of course, they will struggle with this, as sexuality no more defines them than the dust they are made of. It was given to procreate and to express intimacy with another. It was never, ever, meant to be the very definition of who they are or are not.

I truly wish they could see that the breath of God in them is the only thing capable of living up to the weight of their identity.

In the King's service,
Insight

Insight@heaven.edu
Whisper@heaven.edu
Subject: The system is broken.

Dear Whisper,

Your honor bearer is struggling with the school system where he works. He 'naturally' thinks the problem is with the system. He assumes that if he could just fix the system everything would be alright. Because they always start with trying to 'fix' things on the outside, this will be the focus he naturally focuses on. Let me be clear here, systems need to be worked on, but ultimately the problem isn't the system, it is the heart of the people involved. All systems are perfect representations of those involved in them.

Remember how it was for Adam when God was addressing his bad choice? The first thing he did was to blame Eve. Your honor bearer wants to blame the system and all the 'victims' that have been hurt in it.

The reality in their broken world is that all their systems are broken. The first thing each honor bearer must do is own up to their own part in its brokenness. To take ownership at a heart level and change their own thinking and values is the starting place. The only truly good system is the kingdom of our King and it starts in The City. We have perfect systems here because He is our light and the source in every system. They are seeking certainty in a system; get him to focus on certainty in Jesus at a heart level. That is what he is really looking for, he just may not know it fully yet.

In the King's service,
Insight

PS At the end of the notes I will write out some basic thoughts on human systems to help you work with your honor bearer in them.

Whisper@heaven.edu
Insight@heaven.edu
Subject: The Victory

Dear Whisper,

I notice you are trying to figure out what the unfaithful one is doing. You are thinking this is a battle that we still must win. Let me remind you, there is no longer a battle. It is over, finished and completed. Our Beloved's Son has defeated him and settled the matter once and for all. It was never truly about power, as The Sovereign One could have crushed him at any moment. It was his accusation, that our Beloved was not good. That accusation could not be allowed and since he was a high officer in the corps, The Wise One used it as an opportunity to never, ever allow the question to be raised again.

The Wise One answered the question through His own death. When He took His last breath, even The City went dark. We sat, stunned, in utter disbelief that He would have allowed it to happen. All of The City stayed indoors for three days and did nothing, it was a death of our Beloved's Son and we were breathless. We never doubted Him, but we had no idea what He was up to as His Wisdom is so far beyond ours.

On the third day, it was THE DAY, everything changed. We realized the VICTOR had gone to hell and defeated the very kingdom of darkness. He had destroyed the lie of the unfaithful one. Our Beloved was not interested in making a simple statement to defend Himself. He was only interested in crushing the very foundations of the kingdom of darkness and tearing it down, so that never again could it be rebuilt.

The Victor went to hell and destroyed any supposed authority it claimed. He invited those who had lived by faith to join Him and came with all of them to The City to start over.

I know the unfaithful one and his minions are still trying to walk around as if things are normal, but it is all a façade. Don't let your honor bearer get caught up in defeating the minions, it is all about mopping up and building The Kingdom there.

Yes, he should be aware of any last-minute cheap shots the unfaithful one will try as The Victor wraps things up. He is not to be ignored, but also, he is not the focus; The Wise One will help your honor bearer know how to do that in his work.

Keep up the faithfulness.

In the King's service,
Insight

Insight@heaven.edu
Whisper@heaven.edu
Subject: Comfort

Dear Whisper,

I must say, I caught a fresh sense of the pain all around you and it hit me hard. I know I am removed, and it has been a few years since my feet tread on the ashes as you do daily. I felt your tears as they rose before our Father and it touched me deeply. The loss of one of his students through suicide will cut deeply. I am so glad you felt the comfort of our Father for you in your work and our conversation about pain really helped. I trust in these next days he will know the comfort of our Beloved personally and then give it to the parents as well as they walk through it.

I passed the Cherubims last night who are continually before the presence of God. As they receive unending revelation from THE SOURCE, I have found just being next to them puts things back in perspective.

Their crying out, "HOLY, HOLY, HOLY IS THE LORD GOD, THE ALMIGHTY, WHO WAS AND WHO IS AND WHO IS TO COME," after each revelation is like a healing balm. It is like fruit from The Tree by the River, like a walk in the flower gardens, or like a trek in the mountains that surround The City. Our Father has given us so many ways to understand Him and be encouraged, it is hard not to be full and over flowing here. I am reminded of who HE is, and I know HE is at work there in their midst through all the pain going on. We sometimes stand in awe as we watch His Spirit moving back and forth over the earth to strengthen the hearts of all those who will allow Him to.

Of course, I am aware that in the fog of lies down there this might sound like a myth. It is no myth. Nor is it just a symbol as some have claimed. Let me encourage you Whisper, all those ways of our Father to encourage us here are more real than anything you experience down there. Soon, you can return for a break and dip in the stream, eat the fruit, sit by the Cherubim or just sit and enjoy intimacy through a heart to heart conversation.

I look forward to sharing those joys with you.

In the King's service,
Insight

Insight@heaven.edu
Whisper@heaven.edu
Subject: Tension

Dear Whisper,

You mentioned our honor bearer has so many tensions pulling at him and you are concerned for him. His work, you specifically mention his boss, his family, bills, church, wife,… I can't remember how many items you listed, but I get the point. Remember, tension is Our Beloved's idea. Up here, tension is normal and even celebrated. We love tension because there is no power struggle here. In the light, there is nothing to fear in tension because all that is known or can be known is good. Tension reveals new depths to us here. I am reminded of seeing one relationship, where tension deepened the heart of a friend to such a degree that they fell down and worshipped on the spot for what they discovered through it.

Down there tension is seen in a very different 'light'. Even the concept of tension being healthy is beyond their grasp in a dark work. Darkness and tension are two sides of the same coin in their thinking. If there is tension, you can't see the source of it in darkness and it brings up all their fears. I only need to imagine being in a dark room and then hearing or feeling something unusual and the terrifying feelings that can be associated with it in a broken world.

Help your honor bearer to realize that tension is not the problem. He must learn not to fight the tensions as if they are the enemy (remember our discussion of problems and being right, that is the real root of tension that they must deal with). Use the tension between him and his wife or with the students at school to introduce this to him in a safe way. Help him to see that in love, tension is an opportunity to get to know each other (and yourself) better.

Up here, tension is seen as an opportunity through our Father's eyes, but they are so covered up, self-protective and defensive, they automatically assume anything outside of them that unsettles them is the problem.

Help him to see that he doesn't have to fear tension, but slowly teach him to work with it. To listen to it as he might listen to music. Is it a strong beat, fast and pulling him? Is it a subtle tempo with a slow draw to it? Get him used to recognizing the different range of tension and to learn to listen to Our Instructor through it. For She often uses tension as a way to get their attention.

As soon as he accepts the idea that tension is not the problem, he will discover a new freedom to explore life and not have to fix everything. Remind him that life is not a problem to be solved, but a relationship to walk into and explore.

In the King's service,
Insight

Insight@heaven.edu
Whisper@heaven.edu
Subject: Jesus

Dear Whisper,

So many thoughts and images can fill your mind down there. It is easy to get distracted and lose your focus. You wrote last time of your honor bearer not going to church, the tensions at the job, the struggles with his wife. It seems these things are causing him to lose focus on what is truly important.

As one honor bearer said so wisely, 'The most important thing, is to keep the most important thing, the most important thing.' You know well what is most important. There is a fragrance, a sight, a sound, a physical presence that all points to Jesus.

There will be hundreds of weird ideas, theories and doctrines that these broken creatures of dust will position themselves around. They will have arguments, heated arguments that lead to fights just because they all want to be right. They puff up their tiny little chests and stand in their little tiny pulpits and posturize about their tiny little views on their tiny little dark planet, all in the name of majoring on the minors. If it wasn't so terribly sad, it would be funny. Their Sunday messages take so long to say so little they bore me to death. In all fairness, it is a dark world and they are so needy, so let's remind ourselves of our work.

Get your honor bearer to think about, fall in love with, share his life with, get to know intimately and discover in a thousand different ways, the person of Jesus. Not the idea of Jesus, not a theology about Jesus, but the living, breathing, all-encompassing JESUS.

Think of Him as we naturally do here. Ever since THE DAY, we were stunned to see that He has taken on a new 'form', a physical expression of humanity, now the first born of a new creation. He is not bound by this form, but it is as if He has changed his appearance forever because of His love for humanity.

John tried to describe HIM in Revelation, but it fell so far short of the reality. I think, each of us sees HIM a bit differently. As He is the redemption of all life, a finite being cannot begin to grasp the intricacies or complexities of His presence. Each of us sees Him through our own redemption and experiences and in that He comes alive. Then as we share with each other, we grow in our love for Him as seen through others.

It is the same when we see our Beloved, only different. JESUS' life and death as a dust creature somehow opened access to Him that we never dreamed of. Because He experienced being finite, weak and fragile. He owned it in His life lived among them. Because of His experience of life and then death, He knows all of it better than any other being in the universe. He is the first and only GOD/MAN. He is the bridge, the passage, the very conduit through which the honor bearer's life now flows.

Your honor bearer is looking for someone who understands him. Someone who knows the pain of his experiences. Someone who knows how sin has bankrupted him. Someone who has been rejected, cut off and left alone. Someone who can identify at the very core of his heart and not judge him. Someone who will offer him grace and safety in which to deal with his brokenness and be healed.

Teach your honor bearer that Jesus is the ONE he is looking for. HE IS understanding and there is no other. Plant that seed in his spirit, watch over it, keep it the most important thing and everything else will fall into place.

JESUS is Worthy of his life. Everything else is a minor issue than can be worked out with time and grace.

In the King's service,
Insight

Insight@heaven.edu
Whisper@heaven.edu
Subject: Time

I understand your honor bearer is pushing
back against what you are trying to do. As you
said, he sees no problem with little choices of
darkness; taking things from work, lying in his
communication, cheating in small ways, and so
many other areas you have noted.

Yes, he will fight you as a small dust creature
will fight his or her parents. They want their
way and they will fight to get it. When they are
young in the faith, this is normal, but as they
grow -- and your honor bearer has grown a lot
-- he will learn to trust Wisdom more.

What he considers small things in his life, he is
only using his life expectancy as the standard.
So, he sees the ripple effects of the small choice
in the dark over 40 years and assumes it
doesn't matter.

Our Beloved looks at all choices in light of
eternity, not just what it will be in 40 years. He
sees the ugly impact of sin's small choices,
when allowed to multiply over 4,000 years or
even 4,000,000,000,000 years. That is His
standard. All choices are held to an incredibly
high and long standard.

Because our Beloved made us to live forever,
because His Wisdom is complete, He is
concerned about all their choices. Encourage
your honor bearer to see that small

adjustments now, even if they seem insignificant, are vital to learning because if allowed to grow, they become evil beyond the imagination.

God is not a legalist by any stretch of the imagination. He is the most broad and open-minded being in the universe. He is the only being in the universe who has no fears and sees everything for what it is and can be. He will give space and room to experiment in more ways than they can imagine. But he cannot allow deception and rebellion in any moral creation. He has no patience for it because He sees the cost involved. It is a bit like saying, 'How much cancer should we allow?' Just as they will not settle for any cancer, so our Beloved will not allow any darkness.

In the King's service,
Insight

Insight@heaven.edu
Whisper@heaven.edu
Subject: Value personalized

Dear Whisper,

We need to talk about values again as this is
vital to his well-being. If he understood how
valued he is, I would not be going over this
again. The weight of darkness crushes his
sense of value. He assumes his life (being) has
no value. This unquestioned reality is an
overwhelming weight upon him as he knows
in his spirit he 'should' have great value as he
is made in the image of the Almighty. He
assumes his sin has made God value him less.
He lives in the emotional reality of the gap. The
next assumption he makes is that doing things
add value to his being. This results in an
unspoken reality that he is defined by what he
does.

These two assumptions all honor bearers make
are rarely questioned at a deep enough level to
change them. These assumptions become
foundational beliefs for their life. They bring
them into The Kingdom of God and act as if it
is how our Beloved operates. Many of these
honor bearers will live as if this is reality their
whole life, even in their relationship with our
Beloved.

You can see this most clearly when your honor
bearer talks about obedience. He will use the
word obedience as if our Beloved required a
blind and immediate compliance. It is a sign of

immaturity that he will be confronted with daily until he is willing to deal with the issues of the heart. It creates a slavish mentality of passivity of their will, where His will is all about 'doing the right thing'.

You can tell when they are operating from the two assumptions above because when they are obeying the will of God, they feel more valuable. Their passion for the call of God links their value to their obedience. This is nothing more than self-righteousness. They are seeking to please our Beloved without first embracing Jesus. It is legalism and a path that leads to greater brokenness and eventually, death.

Oh, how I wish they would understand, the word 'obedience' at a heart level in our Beloved means nothing more than, listening, paying attention to, giving heed to or understanding. As a child looks to his or her parent, as a servant looks to his or her master, so they are to give heed or pay attention to the Creator of life. Our Beloved knows each of them by name and they have great value to Him. The will of God is not about their value, it is about their relationship to Him. If you love someone, your greatest joy is to find out what pleases them and then doing it as a gift of love.

The Faithful One offers them His righteousness. Now their relationship with The Father can be completely restored and they are to live out of His love. The will of God is expressing this love in their own unique way. The more they know our Beloved's love for them, the less they will be concerned about trying to earn His favor.

In the King's service,
Insight

(P.S. Work is an expression of their value, not a way to get value. Their work has value because they are intrinsically valuable.)

Whisper@heaven.edu
Insight@heaven.edu
Subject: Why is there goodness in the world.

I can see your honor bearer felt stale and superficial in church. He took the risk to seek out depth in a smaller group and that has stirred him up, which is great. Their argument about evil that you wrote me about got me thinking again. They think that if they understand evil, they will be able to deal with it. No surprise there.

I have been thinking a lot about the mystery of wickedness in the world. In his city, he sees violence, greed, depravity and deceit, so it's no wonder he feels the darkness. How different it is here. I just went for a long walk in the mountains yesterday and observed The City far below me. Above it were stars shining in all their glory. As I enjoyed the pure air and dazzling night here, I felt sad about the choking darkness you are confronted with daily. Let me give you my view of the mystery of good and evil.

They are so blinded by the darkness, some see good as evil, and evil as good. They take their best moment, which is very rare, and consider it the 'norm' of their character. They take their worst moment, which is often repeated, and consider it a rare exception. If they were honest, the question would be, 'How come there is goodness in the world?'

For those honor bearers who have no self-awareness at all, they blindly assume that they are good people and goodness is the norm. They are shocked at injustice and evil as if it were an aberration. We know there is no one truly good on the earth and yet...

There is a residue that our Beloved watches over on the earth, it is as if He finds the (rarest) tiniest specks of beauty, goodness and sacrificial love and then goes out of His way to protect, promote and honour it by His Spirit. There is goodness there because our Beloved has not abandoned them and left them to themselves. Take the Spirit of Wisdom from them and they would viciously attack each other.

For those who are honest enough to admit there is evil, many still see humanity -- not God -- as their great hope. I once heard a comedian say, 'The world is good because people are good. If God would just get out of our way, we could do great things and take our place of greatness in the universe.' It brought the house down in its absurdity.

They have no idea how hard our Beloved is at work to bring forth the smallest acts of kindness from the heart in a world that is full of constant back-biting, jealousy, bitterness and arrogance. He will not have to create a hell for them, He will only have to withdraw His presence long enough for their true nature to come forth.

We know as clearly as light can reveal, that there is no goodness that cannot be traced directly to our Beloved at work among them, in spite of them.

In the King's service,
Insight

Whisper@heaven.edu
Insight@heaven.edu
Subject: The power of thanksgiving.

I hope my last email didn't discourage you.
The evil there will cause your honor bearer to
feel discouragement, frustration and
disappointment. Everywhere he goes, he will
be confronted with his own limitations and
brokenness. I know you feel the pain of this for
him so here is a small thing to do which has
great power.

Teach him the discipline of giving thanks.

Sin causes a loss of perspective and
discontentment with life itself. The clearest
'Fruit' of darkness is the grumbling of
ungratefulness. It is that attitude of heart that
says, 'I can't get enough of what I want and
what I want is all that matters.' Discontent
breeds darkness and multiplies human misery
like maggots in death.

We must teach them there, the small things that
we take for granted here. In The City, gratitude
is as natural as fruit hanging from the tree of
life, as color in the gardens at the entrance to
The City or as wetness is to the stream flowing
through The City. Everything we have we have
been given. We didn't earn it and feel no need
to. Our Beloved is All Powerful and has infinite
resources. His greatest joy is giving, and we
receive it and then give it away as we can.

He doesn't require us to give thanks, as that would be like Him requiring us to breathe. We do it because it is the one thing we can give in return for all He is and does for us. Everything we do and are is a reflection of thankfulness.

We build, create, teach, grow and serve, all as simple expressions of this gratefulness. Teach your honor bearer, in all things, to give thanks, for our Beloved is at work, even in the darkest times, to bring forth things that your honor bearer can't even imagine.

We can't begin to explain the glory of life here, it is unspeakable in their dark world. Teach him that giving thanks for small things will keep sickness, discouragement and discontent at a distance and go a long way towards giving him the life he truly desires.

In the King's service,
Insight

Whisper@heaven.edu
Insight@heaven.edu
Subject: Arrogance

Dear Whisper,

I love the note you wrote, "I long to pull out
my sword and cut the chains that hold them
captive here. I saw one man standing in front
of a large mirror in a weight room. He had
worked hard to build up his muscles, and he
admired each one. Vanity! And arrogance too!
If only he could see himself from our side. In
turning to the flesh instead of the Spirit for
power, that withered soul only chained himself
more firmly to the darkness.

Unless the honor bearers embrace the light,
nothing will change. You can cut away areas of
bondage, but if the change is not their choice,
they only become more arrogant and driven to
hide and defeat the 'light' that they think made
them feel so bad.

Arrogance is an attitude that says 'light' is the
problem. It is an attitude or way of thinking
that says, I will define what is right, good and
valuable on my own terms. It rails against any
'light' they cannot control and anything that
makes them look bad.

The arrogance of the unfaithful one is that he thinks
himself wiser than the Almighty. He takes on
the exalted role of judging God for doing
things differently. In his thinking, 'how dare

God do things different than what I think is right?'

When our Beloved works in a way he disagrees with, he takes it on himself to 'expose' it and then seeks to belittle and destroy God for disagreeing with him.

The unfaithful one loves to focus on his rights rather than his responsibilities. He abuses the freedom given him and then attacks our Beloved for being irresponsible in granting humans such freedom. All of this produces a hardness of heart. He is militantly ignorant against any issues that expose his heart.

Here is how you can recognize his presence at work in the broken honor bearers:
*   They say God is not good (An easier way to say it is His fault). God messed up and it is the responsibility of 'good' people to question Him.
*   The fruit of blaming God is they can then justify being pawns or victims in the world God created. It is not their fault (God is to blame).
*   The fruit of this is self-pity. They are victims and should really be pitied as it is not their fault.
*   As there is no good 'authority', this means they are easily consumed with what people think about them as they are the only authority.
*   The darkened reasoning then leads them to take on the role of judge and jury against anyone or anything they don't like. They belittle anyone who disagrees with their "right" perspective.

*	They hate anyone who has something they don't or can't have.
*	As they are the authority, they are driven to control things and rail against anything they can't control.
*	Finally, the unfaithful one hates weakness. He is all about power. That is truly all they care about.

(The only other option for the above is to deny God and say He doesn't exist. They then find life as meaningless and the argument above goes through the same basic process.)

Now even as I write these things, we here in The City now see clearly that these ideas are ridiculous, foolish, utterly ludicrous and outrageous. As you can see, I can't find the words to explain how arrogant they are. But, here is the challenge, the unfaithful one is at work right now creating darkness in which these ideas might, just might, seem possible to the foolish.

Sadly, you will see these attributes in anyone who will not walk with humility into the light of the Humble One. But here is my counsel, don't focus on him. Let Wisdom and The Victor deal with him, just recognize the roots of evil at work and teach your honor bearer the ways of our Beloved, and none of this will take root in him.

In the King's service,
Insight

Whisper@heaven.edu
Insight@heaven.edu
Subject: God's right to rule

Dear Whisper,

I am glad to hear the honor bearer is continually engaged in the study of our Beloved's written Word. Hopefully, he will continue to find support and friendship and wisdom in that small group. A small safe group to listen and be listened to can't be over rated as a part of his maturing.

It seems so obvious here that being fully submitted to Him is the most natural thing. To think otherwise is a bit like a bird thinking about air for its wings, or a fire thinking about the wood that fuels it. So, let me state what we 'know', and you might use this as an ongoing reference point there. *God is God and they are not.* To even write such words feels like I have reduced language to grunts and groans, but you have asked me for the basics, and that expresses the very basics of our relationship.

To put it as simply as possible, our Beloved has an obligation, a responsibility to rule over all of creation. He is duty bound to lead us. As He brought us all into being, He is obligated to maintain our being and watch over us. He does this with such grace that here in The City we feel an extraordinary security.

The image that comes to mind is the throne of God at the heart of The City. Do you remember it Whisper? Walking into the great hall, feeling the rush of a mighty wind pulling you toward the source of all life.

Mercy meets you at the doorway, making sure you are presentable. Her eyes are intense, cleansing anything unclean. She kisses you gently on the forehead and in a strange sense, you know that mark is required to enter further.

Grace welcomes you in a strong but deferential way. She will not push her way on anyone entering but when she holds out her arm and you take it, you feel like you're in the presence of a life-long friend you have known from the first moment you took a breath.

Remember how the winds slowly change as Grace steps into the Hallway of Presentation. Those winds leaving become less and those returning become stronger. It is as if the winds are His very Word, returning with joy to speak of what they have accomplished.

You begin to feel the weight of His glory. With each step, the presence of the Sovereign One becomes clearer and heavier. Our Beloved is the most real, 'HEAVY' being in the universe. He weighs on you as you get close to Him. None can stand in His presence. His glory is reality and He is the heaviest substance in the universe. As His glory becomes clearer you feel the weight of it, and you have to focus on just holding yourself up. You actually wonder if you should or could continue without being crushed.

Then you notice colors springing into life all around you, they are not just definitions of light, they are actual beings, created by HIM and for HIM. They are dancing around in a symphony of glory that is unimaginable. Fragments of colors breaking off, exploding and then returning to the primary color. Millions upon millions of them at a cellular level, creating images of beauty and majesty in celebrations of color.

Then you notice the sounds of all nature coming alive all around you. All the materials of the hall, the gold, jewels, building stones, pearls and fabrics over the windows and hanging on the walls start out as a whisper. That is where you got your name! There is harmony and melody, and every imaginable sound. Like the moment they were spoken into existence, they are declarations of beauty, woven into a glorious orchestra.

Then you see HIM. It is as if the hall ceases to exist. For nothing competes with HIS presence. As all things point to HIM, as soon as the colors and the sounds notice you turning your attention to HIM, they become quiet, silenced, so as not to distract you. For how could HIS glory compete with the source of all glory?

It is only in that raw moment, where you are exposed, known and revealed, that you realize

Grace is holding you together in HIS presence…

Forgive me Whisper, for I fear I am making you desperately home sick and ruining you for the work there in the dark lands. I got caught up in trying to describe it and forgot it will be a faint memory there. All I can say is that on your return to HIS Presence you will be held, cleaned and comforted by HIM for your service as you re-orientate yourself to The City.

Now I say all that in light of your question. Who is worthy to take the seat on the throne of the universe? Truly, only HE who WAS and WHO IS and WHO IS TO COME can do it.

Can you imagine one of those dear little dust creatures trying to crawl up onto the throne of the universe? They cannot hold themselves together. How absurd of them to think they could hold the universe together.

Whisper, please help your honor bearer to grasp that he is not God. This will give them freedom to be truly human.

In the King's service,
Insight

Whisper@heaven.edu
Insight@heaven.edu
Subject: Guilt

Dear Whisper,

It is not surprising that a question about
feelings of guilt would arise after our earlier
discussion about emotions. You are right to
raise it and see how important it is for these
dust beings who we are called to serve. They
never question the pleasure side of emotions
and assume they are natural and good. They
cannot make the connection that to experience
the pleasure side of emotions, they must
include the pain side of them as well. They all
come through the same channel.

To fully help clarify what guilt is, we must take
a step back and look at choice, freedom or the
will. The Blessed Three have enjoyed
relationship for longer than we could imagine.
This relationship, in their eternal wisdom, was
the source of their greatest joy, celebration and
the purest pleasure that was possible for them.
They took the risk and created smaller beings
who have the same capacity for relationship. A
mystery that is truly wonderful.

To create these finite beings with a free will but
no guidance or sense of responsibility would
have been the cruelest joke possible. Our
Beloved would never do that. These little
creatures of dust would have spent all their
time making foolish choices because they
would not know better. Their choices would
have been the source of unmeasurable pain. In
language you can use to help your honor

bearer, they have a disease called Leprosy. It is when they can't feel anything through the infected skin or parts of their body. They then hurt themselves because of the loss of awareness. In the same way, guilt was given to help them keep connected to their world and learn from their mistakes.

So, The Wise One gave them a guidance system, which we talked about earlier, values. God recognized that they needed to trust Him to know what was best, so He kept it very simple. He gave them a raw choice. Do not eat of this fruit. It was not magical fruit, it just gave them a very concrete way of expressing their trust in Him as the source of all wisdom.

A part of free will, a gift included with the process, is that they would include the pleasure of good choices. A healthy choice produces enjoyable emotions.

Guilt is the natural response of a creature who has seen a greater value and refuses it. God gave them the capacity to feel guilt as a way to show them the foolishness of this choice and to then learn from it.

All emotions have a purpose. The question is not whether I like it or not, the question is what behavior was it meant to encourage? Guilt was given to help them understand that they did something wrong and must change or repent of the choice they have made.

In the King's service,
Insight

Whisper@heaven.edu
Insight@heaven.edu
Subject: Does might make right?

Dear Whisper,

No, I don't mind your many questions. The one you posed about God's leadership of these little ones is the most basic question any moral being can ask.

Might does not make right. Just because the Almighty is powerful, that does not automatically give Him the right to rule. I know the children of dust will make this an excuse to justify their rebellion, but people looking for an excuse will always find one.

If might makes right, then our Beloved would be a control freak (to use their language). He would be interested in pulling all power to himself. But we know, we see every day that He loves to empower creation and even gives people there more space than they know what to do with.

It only becomes a true right or obligation to rule when it is seen in His value. His infinite power, when matched with His Character (love and goodness), make it the full expression of value. Who He is – His character and nature – are what give Him the moral responsibility to rule. He is the most valuable being in the universe and uses that (we call it glory) as the divine touching point for reality.

When these creatures of dust only see His power, what they create is a focus on religion. They focus on what they can do to appease this powerful being and false religion is born.

This is your work. This is the fullest expression of your focus. It is the hardest seed to plant in their heart but plant it you must. For once they see that HE is worthy, that His very being, His essence, is the most valuable 'thing' in the universe, the freedom this brings cannot be put into words. For from it flows repentance, humility and grace.

A clear way to put this in perspective is to go back to the email and look at Jesus and His willingness to empty Himself and live among them and then die in their place. No power-hungry God would ever even consider that, but it was His joy to break the lie of the unfaithful one, once and for all. Yes, God rules in part because He is all powerful; in addition to this, He rules from the heart, because He is good.

In the King's service,
Insight

Whisper@heaven.edu
Insight@heaven.edu
Subject: Repentance

Dear Whisper,

Here, in The City, we have never tasted the drink of rebellion, but they are drunk with it. What we do naturally, in great joy, they now must do as a conscious, disciplined choice. They must acknowledge they are not God and He is. That means they must lay down their rebellious heart and surrender to Him.

For us here when the Savior is present, it is the most natural thing to kneel. It truly is a step of humility to not kneel, but to keep standing that we might more quickly do His bidding. It seems the very opposite for them. They resist, they fight, they seek distraction for anything but kneeling before Him. But know this, kneel they must. It is not an option. They are not making Him "LORD", they are only acknowledging what He has been all along.

This first step is called repentance and is vital to any relationship with our Beloved. They stole their life from Him, they are thieves. They have trampled on His glory, they are arrogant fools. They fight His light as if it is their enemy. They would kill the Almighty again if given the chance. Of all this they must repent and kneel before the Sovereign or face the consequences.

The thought of standing before Him without the kiss of Mercy or Grace holding onto you is terrifying. It is the terror of all terrors and make it as clear as you can that they do not want to feel the wrath of the Judge as a result of the actions stated above. For truly they would be exposed and thus, undone.

In the King's service,
Insight

Whisper@heaven.edu
Insight@heaven.edu
Subject: A cause for celebration

Dear Whisper,

I rejoice with you at the changes taking place in your honor bearer. You watch over the ember slowly glowing in him. You try and highlight what we have been talking about and carry him in your heart. You wonder, day by day, if or when it will burst into flames and then when it does, it is truly a cause for celebration. How and when it happens, is truly a mystery, but such a joy, in our work, nothing compares to it.

He has humbled himself to his wife and shared about his own pain in growing up with his mother and the reserve he had growing in him towards his wife because of not dealing with his mother. He realized he was hiding from his boss as well and was playing the victim in that relationship. The tears of his sharing with his wife and a willingness to own his own life are truly a healing salve to all of us. I only wish I could have seen the smile on our Beloved's face when this happened.

This step of living faith is key for his growth. He has experienced truth in his inner being. He has taken the risk and voiced issues going on inside of himself. He named the emotions and brought them into the light in a conversation of love.

This will bring forth an emotional high that he will be able to ride for a season. He will be hungry for more truth and life in his relationships. Encourage him to share this breakthrough with others in his small group as it will encourage them in their own walk.

As much as he feels good now, we both know the deeper revelation and intimacy will bring forth new challenges for him. You don't need to bring them up for a while, but we both know they are coming as any personal breakthrough will also expose others around him who have grown comfortable and who will push back and not want him to change too much as it will expose them.

As in all seasons, this 'spring' in his life will produce fruit that many will enjoy. There are other winters coming that will challenge him in new ways and also new springs as that is the beauty of life in their world.

Good work Whisper, you have worked well, and we can see the fruit of it in his life.

In the King's service,
Insight

Whisper@heaven.edu
Insight@heaven.edu
Subject: The unfaithful one

Dear Whisper,

I commend you for helping the honor bearer to admit weakness. Being vulnerable or appearing out of control is something the unfaithful one hates. I am so glad you were able to plant the seed that our Beloved is Worthy in that humbled heart. Now you will be amazed how natural it is for him to glorify our Beloved.

A wise one once said, 'The chief end of man is to glorify God and enjoy Him forever.' Glory is not what He demands, as if He needs anything from them. They glorify Him by simply walking in the light. We just call it life. All energy flows from Him and as it does not return void, it returns with the bounty of produce and that is the glory due Him from all of life.

Because so many in that dark and foggy world think they can author all arguments, all growth and development within themselves, they assume they are 'gods', and they then naturally assume their role is to glorify self. They can no more be 'gods' than the unfaithful one. Here the image is seared into our minds of when he raised his fist up and declared himself equal to God. The defiance, the arrogance, the blasphemy of it still shocks us to this day.

Some have said he was chased from heaven, but I think all our Father had to do was give Him The Look, and he fled for his life. The unfaithful one presumed he would be judged on the spot. He hoped to prove our Beloved was insecure and would never allow anyone to disagree with Him. Instead our Beloved has given him space, even before his throne, to speak and live out his argument.

The unfaithful one grows smaller, darker and more desperately foolish with each passing season. He is left with one purpose -- to try to persuade creation that our Beloved is not good. He answered the unfaithful one with such clear certainty in Jesus, none will ever question Him again.

In the King's service,
Insight

Whisper@heaven.edu
Insight@heaven.edu
Subject: Is love a feeling?

Dear Whisper,

Time has passed and your honor bearer has settled into life again. Yes, your honor bearer's confusion over whether love must be accompanied by feelings is a common question. The dust creatures were made to live out of their heart. Their head was given as a support system to define matters of the heart so they could be shared in words. He will have experienced the emotional high of intimacy that touches him in his deepest parts. He will secretly hope that it never goes away, but the feelings of it will ebb and flow as is very natural in their world.

The ability to feel and thus experience the world is a brilliantly simple gift of the Creator, but they have lost all perspective because of their darkness of heart. Love is a choice that goes beyond feelings. There will be times when the honor bearer feels great love for his wife, like when she flashes those hazel eyes at him. Most times his love for her is just there, steady but not at all emotional. So, it must be with our love for the Almighty One. Observe how emotional he is when singing a worship song he loves. When he isn't feeling that, he wonders whether he truly loves our Beloved.

Human feelings are so muddled and disturbed. The dust creatures are absorbed with them but will not go deep to understand why they are there. They simply refuse to look at the values beneath their feelings.

It is a bit like trying to put out a fire by trying to blow the smoke away. The more you blow on the fire, the hotter and stronger it becomes and the more smoke it produces. You have to deal with the values in order to truly understand emotions.

Remember, God is the most valuable being in the universe. He created us all in love and our hearts were made to discover that love and respond. To repeat what I said above, love is a choice rooted in value. The way to understand the values at work is to learn to 'speak' the language of values, which is emotions.

You will need to remind him periodically that God's presence in his life is not a feeling, but a covenantal commitment from God. He has declared it with words, our Beloved will not fail or forsake him. Once spoken, our Beloved's words are as certain as He is.

God's presence with them is not really complicated, but for them it is a disciplined part or choice of life to walk in.

In the King's service,
Insight

Whisper@heaven.edu
Insight@heaven.edu
Subject: Holiness

Dear Whisper,

You do ask many clarifying questions and I must admit, I love them. When I read, 'Is holiness optional?' I was a bit stunned. I would never, ever think to look at it that way. I know just by the question how you are struggling with your honor bearer and his view of holiness. So, let me see if I can state the obvious, at least from how we live here.

These dear honor bearers have reduced the life of God to a religious activity. They will not deal with the heart, and just want to do the right thing. Holiness to them means they are 'doing' the right things and are safe.

I will step back and look at the bigger picture of our Beloved's intent and hopefully it helps you know how to work with your dust bunny.

When our Beloved created them, He set apart the seventh day as Holy. It was a day set apart to cease from working. As He had given them six days to fill with their own vocation, He commanded them to take one day a week to set apart for Him.

Holiness was meant to be space set aside for the presence of God, intimacy and reflection, to be woven into their life. After the great rebellion, our Beloved gave them a tabernacle in which His presence would dwell. It even had a 'holy of holies,' space set apart for Him to dwell.

Now, fast forward to our Jesus and His incredible humility, going to live among them. He changed everything. He went back to the heart or motive of His Father in all He did.

He took their sin upon himself, so they might be holy again. Not in what they do, but in who they are. He sent the Spirit of Empowerment and Wisdom to them to empower them to live this life.

Now they don't have to worry about making space for God on a certain day, or in a certain location, but they make space for Him in their heart on a moment by moment basis. Holiness is the space they give for God to dwell in them through the gift of Jesus.

Holiness is meant to be that space made for the Infinite Pure One to dwell in their heart. It is a heart set apart from self as a sacrifice of thanksgiving. Now you can ask the question, 'Is holiness optional?'

Of course, NO. It is the very essence of the message and training we are involved in. As He dwells in their hearts, the most natural fruit will be their growing likeness to His purity by being pure themselves. It is not something they do as a starting place, it is the fruit of His presence in them.

I trust that every short overview gives you perspective and reminds you of the heart of The Father for His creation.

In the King's service,
Insight

Whisper@heaven.edu
Insight@heaven.edu
Subject: Good News

Dear Whisper,

Congratulations. I just heard that you were being promoted. You will be overseeing a group of leaders who will be working together in their city. Your current honor bearer will be handed over to another angel, but rest assured you will always be updated on how he is doing and his growth. I know you will always be interested in working with him and his family in the years ahead and we will always keep you informed on his process.

On another note, you will be coming home for a short stay. I am so excited to get to see you and spend hours catching up. These emails are okay, but they lack the intimacy and depth of sharing we are so used to here. I will arrange a welcome home dinner amongst our friends. Please come ready to share your heart with us.

You will also have days of restoration and renewal here and we will give you space to 'catch your breath' in regard to the beauty and joy of The City. I heard there is a new musical being put together by a group of honor bearers that want to express the joy of their arrival here and the opening will be the day after you arrive. I will get us seats for sure.

You will now need to understand systems at work and the dynamics of group life among the honor bearers. I will include notes on my thinking as a part of getting you ready for this new adventure. It will give you a sense of overview and if you have time, think about it and come with lots of questions so that we can interact and get you started in your new role of nation building.

I look forward to your coming with great joy.

In the King's service,
Insight

Whisper@heaven.edu
Insight@heaven.edu
Subject: Systems at work

Dear Whisper,

If you stood back and looked at my writing, you might be tempted to think it is all about the individual. As if their salvation is all that matters. I fear the last 100 to 200 years have set things up so that in their modern religious activities, this is all they can think about. I must say it is a bit like being focused on the birth of a child and then once born, forgetting about how to raise them.

What makes a child mature is a healthy family system.

What makes a citizen mature is a healthy governmental system.

What makes a believer mature is a healthy religious system.

It isn't a question I can answer here, but it is the same old human question, 'Which comes first, the chicken or the egg?' If there is a broken system, it is hard for an individual to mature. Of course, our Beloved can bring growth in any human, in any circumstances, but without mature individuals the system can't maintain its health. It is a dilemma our Beloved left humanity so they might learn to seek Him to learn His ways. As we have talked about the individual in the last notes, now we need to look at how to create strong systems so that the community and nation might grow up as well. As a teacher, your honor bearer needs to value his students as individuals but to help them see themselves as part of a learning community.

Before I end these notes (they have grown much longer than I intended), I will put my thoughts down on what our Beloved calls, Discipling the Nations. For this is very close to Wisdom's heart and we must be faithful to share the whole counsel of our Beloved and not just pick out the stuff we like doing.

In the King's service,
Insight

Whisper@heaven.edu
Insight@heaven.edu
Subject: Containers

Dear Whisper,

In the transition that lies ahead for you. You will be shifting your focus from working with an individual, to working with individuals who are part of a system. This new thinking and awareness will be vital to your thinking about building a system there in which the Spirit of Wisdom can maximize a way for them to 'hold' who our Beloved is in their midst.

There is much confusion and misunderstanding there regarding institutions (I will use the word institution, organization. container and system interchangeably in these notes. We can talk about why when you get there). Our Beloved has divine purposes for institutions just as he does for individuals. Think of systems as containers. To understand this, we must go back to what was in the heart of our Beloved when He gave dust creatures the desire to create something bigger than themselves. If they don't understand God's intention, they will be forever confused with organizations.

In creating Adam, He took the dust of the earth and breathed into this shell or vessel His life. The key image we know from The City is that we are containers of life, not creators of life.

That means we 'hold' what He has given to us, we don't create it.

Then He creates Eve, but now out of the vessel called Adam. She was in Adam but was taken from him so that he would know he (and she) is complete in himself, but incomplete alone. In this relationship a new 'container' is born. Their relationship with each other will create something new, different from each individual. The sum of their relationship will be greater than each individual. This new container (a relational system) is what our Beloved calls marriage. As time goes on in the story of our Beloved, He creates several key systems in which to hold His glory in their midst.

Now as I have said many times, but will say it one last time, this is so normal and a part of life here in The City that we don't even think about it. Here we create groups or little communities (relational containers) that hold a particular revelation of our Beloved. There is one for certain flowers, groups of flowers and even gardens. There are many for food and eating. There are hundreds of them around areas of interest (revelation of our Beloved) that they get together and create and hold a particular insight into how the Creator works. Each one is unique and holds through their relationships a beauty that is unique to them.

Let me go back to our conversation of life there in the dark world. This was our Beloved's original purpose. If you don't understand the above, any group or community will be very confusing for them. They will think it is all about them and they will compete to 'fill' the containers meant for the glory of God with all kinds of their own self-destructive emptiness. Of course, they implode because they have no real glory of the Creator to hold.

Our Beloved longs for these systems to truly represent Him to the world. Governments were meant to hold revelation of His justice. Education was meant to be a container that would hold revelation of His wisdom. Arts, sports and entertainment were meant to hold expressions of His beauty and the celebration of challenge. As we said above, the family or marriage is to hold the beauty of intimacy as a safe place for children. Science and technology was meant to hold understanding of the material world and how it works.

Another vital container we see our Beloved telling them about is the Body of Christ. Another more intimate word used to describe this container is The Bride of Christ. This container is meant to hold the collected revelations of purity, transparency and wholeness as seen in the only true source of it, Our Beloved.

My dear Whisper, my friend, this revelation has been lost in their dark world. They only see institutions as bureaucratic, greedy, arrogant and unconcerned about the individual. There are some that are just pure evil, taken over and empowered by people whose only loyalty is greed flamed by the unfaithful one.

143

Your new honor bearers will long to create something greater than themselves. That is as natural to him as existence is. It will come through relationships. Teach him to build relationships within the purposes of our Beloved and he will see things that will be truly glorious in their broken and dark world.

In the King's service,
Insight

Questions that would be relevant in your work.
What is the agreed-on purpose for the group existing?
All containers exist to do something.
What values are vital to the system's existence?
What character expression of God (glory) would this container hold?
How can you build all this into the heart of the leaders, so they model it to all involved?
The leaders must take it to heart themselves and live it as without this they will try and fill the container with their own 'glory'.

Whisper@heaven.edu
Insight@heaven.edu
Subject: Getting the system 'right'

Dear Whisper,

Before I introduce my more detailed notes, I
am reminded of something that you must be
very careful of in training up your leadership
team there.

One of the most basic assumptions they make
about institutions is that if they can get it
'right', then everything will be alright (I said
this above, but it bears repeating here). They
think in a perfect 'system' everyone won't have
to worry about being good, they will just be
carried by the current of the system and all will
be well. This is foolishness in a broken world.
As we have said, they will have to fight the
currents of the systems of their world in order
to grow up. There is no other life offered them.

Their assumption is that the problem is outside
of themselves and so they blame the system for
their own brokenness. Don't let them build on
this assumption because it leads to people
being victims of the system and leaders then
quickly assuming 'control' over the system in
order to 'fix' the people.

On a deeper level, there are no perfect or
broken systems strictly speaking. All systems
are created and represent the values and beliefs
of the people who start them and maintain
them. You can't and will never have perfect

relational systems in a broken world because of the broken people involved. That is why we spend so much time in all our earlier emails trying to get you clear on how to work in the heart of the honor bearer.

One more side note is important and I want you thinking about it before you come, and we can talk it all out. The biggest challenges your leaders will face is the speed of change going on around them. So, there will be naturally lots of talk about creating a relational system that can handle the speed of change. The important point is that as your honor bearers work to change the relational containers, or another way of saying it is to 'disrupt the systems', others won't like the changes and will sabotage them. Any time a leader or person in a relational system starts to change themselves, it will always, always make others feel vulnerable and the easiest thing for them to do is blame the 'change agent' and verbally tear them down and try to get them to be back to being what they used to be like so that they feel safe in a stable system. So, beware as you work with leaders, this is coming as sure for them as the air they breathe.

In the King's service,
Insight

Questions that would be relevant in your work.

Where is there tension in the system?

The tension is not the problem, it is simply the point where a conversation needs to take place because of a lack of clarity, goals, expectations or understanding.

Be aware that the tension points will be key areas where change is needed.

How is / are your leader/s handling the tension and are they framing it as a problem or a dilemma?

Where are they? Who are they listening to? What are they responsible for? (These should take you back to what we talked about earlier in regard to the questions our Beloved asks.)

Who is trying to change and where will those around him or her try and counter it and stop them from feeling vulnerable? (Work hard not to let the leaders take the push back as personal.)

Whisper@heaven.edu
Insight@heaven.edu
Subject: Spheres of authority

Dear Whisper,

As you continue to think about key institutions the honor bearers are trying to build there in their dark world, you will realize a fundamental question will need to be clear for them, so it needs to be clear in your own thinking in working with them. The issue is the understanding of authority. Who has the Beloved's delegated authority to do what?

Our Beloved's vulnerability means He has genuinely delegated power and responsibility to people and the systems or institutions they create. This is the most basic reality we angels deal with. Our Creator made space in which another's will can be done and not His. The whole essence of darkness is that someone's will, other than our Beloved's, is being done. That is the very definition of darkness. Our Beloved is light and where His will is not being done is darkness and death.

We angels were naïve ourselves at the beginning. The first-time authority became a question was when the unfaithful one stood against The Almighty. He raised his fist against the will of our Beloved and summoned us to follow Him rather than the Humble One. This opened a time of warfare that continues to this day. Even our warriors who go fight the unfaithful one and his minions are careful about authority in everything they do.

As you develop your thinking about systems, there will be four key institutions needed for building a nation. They are points of authority that you and your honor bearers need to understand and learn to work within. I will list them below and the tension points needed to keep them healthy.

Individual
Each honor bearer is made in the image of our Beloved. That means they carry His stamp of authority to create with their choices a path expressing who they are. With this delegated authority comes a responsibility of stewardship. This authority was given to each person so there would be millions of unique expressions of our Beloved. Each with the capacity to create beauty and joy from the heart. Our Beloved has such a deep respect for them that He will knock on the door of each heart, but He will not break it down in the name of His will being done. Each honor bearer is accountable directly to our Beloved for who he or she is and their choices.

Please note that each individual has great value because they are made in the image of our Beloved. Each of the following three systems can only function when this revelation is clearly in the heart of each honor bearer. If your honor bearers lose this or those following them lose it, the systems below will collapse in a short time.

Government

Honor Bearers are given the freedom to create a government to rule over them. Our Beloved knew structures of justice would be needed to build a safe place for people to live and work. He wanted His people to create an institution that would hold 'evil' in check. This container is meant to hold an ongoing revelation of our Beloved's justice. In essence, as stated above, each individual has value and thus a system must be created to watch over it and guard that value.

This is a bottom up structure. The authority comes to the government system through the people. Governments can control the people some of the time, but ultimately the people will control the destiny of the government. The mandate from society is to create an even playing field for as many of the dust creatures as possible.

Family

The family container has authority over their children and their home, which includes stewardship of their finances and property. Their delegated authority is established to provide the means in which traditions and values can be passed to the next generation. This is a limited top down structure. It is limited in that the parents don't have authority over their children forever.

Our Beloved has said the husband is to model self-sacrificing love and the wife is to model respect. Both are the basis of intimacy and give the children a preparation or lens in which to see Our Beloved (We talked about this in the earlier emails so hopefully it makes sense to you here). They both have co-responsibility over their children. These little honor bearers are required to honor their parents in their life.

Church
This is a top down delegated authority which is limited to moral authority. It is an authority that operates within the framework that our Beloved has revealed through His Word. The standard is one of mercy and grace rooted in revelational love. Our Beloved will personally hold the leaders in His church accountable to the Word. The honor bearers who attend church are free to come and go as they sense the will of our Beloved for them.

The container called the Church always has the right and obligation to model the highest moral authority within society. They don't have the right to legislate it (That is the will of the people through government). No one can tell a pastor or religious leader you don't have the right to live this standard, but the pastor has no right to judge people if they don't live the same standard as he does. The standard which you ought to live morally by, is set by Our Beloved, and hopefully modeled by the rest of the Body of Christ.

As you will quickly see, there is tension between these areas that will require some serious communication and heartfelt understanding of the wisdom of Our Beloved.

Let me say again, if we had not worked for so long in our personal friendship and our emails, I would not even bother to send you these notes as they only truly make sense and work if you have laid the foundation shared in all the communications above.

In the King's service,
Insight

Questions that would be relevant in your work.

Which institution does your leadership team work in and how can they model it in their relationships?

Who do you need them to work with and support to build checks and balances in the authority systems at work? (There will be specific questions in each of the domains that will help them be clear on who is responsible for what. We can talk about them when you get back.)

Where are their weaknesses in the system and who do you need to build or mature in order to make the system stronger?

Where are the tension points between the spheres of authority and how is your leadership team responding to them?

Whisper@heaven.edu
Insight@heaven.edu
Subject: The nation as a whole

Dear Whisper,

As the honor bearers you will be working with
in your next mission are all leaders in the
community, let me assume that you will
quickly realize there is more to a community
that just the four areas listed above. So, to keep
your thinking moving forward in preparation
for your time here and all the questions going
through your mind, let me quickly add that
there are other relational containers in a nation.
I mentioned the four above because they have
a delegated authority from our Beloved. These
below relational systems will have to fit in and
work with the four systems mentioned above.

Education
This sphere has to do with our dear Wisdom
and how she works. It is not the downloading
of information but building the capacity in
children in how to grow up and learn to
celebrate the world our Beloved made and
how it works. This area fits clearly under the
authority of the family who has primary
responsibility for the children and how they
grow up.

Arts and entertainment
This sphere has to do with beauty and re-
creation. It celebrates many different
expressions and cultures. It is a gifting our
Beloved put in those precious ones who call

the world to attention, to show something in a new, enduring way. Much like a poet, all artists take the mundane and reorganize it to capture a new expression of wonder and mystery. The best of it holds people's attention and reminds them of our Beloved. Those "artists" there who try to create without His light produce only darkness and ugly sensuality. As hard as they try, one day they will realize there is no beauty outside of our Beloved.

Communication

This is the glue that holds all the domains together. As Our Beloved's spoken Word created all life, so the honor bearers' spoken word maintains the life of any group or community. A group that can communicate effectively can learn to express their true purpose in this world. These give the clearest picture of who Our Beloved is and who we are supposed to be.

There is a formula that says the capacity of a relational system to deal with challenges, to learn and thus maintain an ongoing effectiveness is equal to their capacity to communicate effectively about the issues, tensions and conflicts that arise along the way.

Each honor bearer is responsible for their communication choices. The best choices are informed choices, those with a reverence for truth. Look around there Whisper, and you will see there are no developed countries that don't have freedom of expression. There are no highly developed countries that stifle communication. Jesus never tried to silence anyone, he only demanded the right to bring his own message. The only voices he ever silenced where the minions and they were telling the truth. The revelation of our Beloved to the honor bearers in this relational system is that He is the living Word.

Science and technology
This is the relational system that deals with the physical world. Those who study the Earth in all its vast molecular detail or the worlds beyond the Earth have ample evidence of our Beloved's existence. He set in place laws, order and patterns of life so they could be understood. This reality gives humanity a place to understand their choices in concrete terms. Using our Beloved's resources and abilities, they have created technologies that have produced much good but also much evil. Science gives them the most practical way to see the consequences of their choices and learn from them if they will.

In the King's service,
Insight

Questions that would be relevant in your work.

A 'nation' is not just a political entity in one sense, or boundaries on a map, it is a group of people who own their identity and group together to form a union in which containers must be built to hold the glory of our Beloved.

What are the unique expressions of our Beloved that define this relational system?

A vital container above is communication. It is the easiest way to measure the maturity of all the people involved in the relational system. Where are their tension points and are they able to talk at a deep enough level to deal with the issues?

Whisper@heaven.edu
Insight@heaven.edu
Subject: Choices that destroy a nation

Dear Whisper,

As I wrap up my thinking with these notes, I
thought I would look at what choices will
destroy a nation. These are potentially raw
areas that the history of the dark planet has
shown them to be very susceptible to. They
seem obvious to us, but as we have said over
and over, the things that are obvious to us are
great revelation to them. As a starting point,
lack of each person dealing with their own
heart issues is a given in this. As they say, one
rotten apple can spoil a whole barrel of apples,
but as we are talking about relational systems
here, I will stick to the big issues we see from
the story of our Beloved at work.

Political injustice.
A government is to represent the Kingdom of
Our Beloved by creating laws that are just and
good for all. They are boundary keepers who
limit the expression of brokenness in a society.
When a government creates law or
manipulates its power to only benefit the elite,
rich or a chosen few, it is the beginning of the
end for the nation as the corruption will kill the
honor bearers until all that is left is anarchy,
totalitarianism or they cease to exist and are
taken over by another nation.

Economic injustice.
When honor bearers cannot make a living wage, when there are no jobs, when there is no ability to sustain a family by working, it destroys a nation. One of the primary ways of the provision for life is through a healthy economy. When the rich own most of the natural resources and have no social responsibility, a nation will slowly die as the honor bearers will lose heart and resort to their brokenness to deal with the pain.

Sexual perversion and the destruction of the family.
The family is the building block of any community or nation. It is the foundation out of which healthy children can be brought up. Destroy the family unit and you destroy the generations to come as they have no sense of belonging, love or safety. If you take away the family, the next generation will be angry, bitter and alone, and take it out on all those around them.

Misuse of their words to create their own distorted reality.
They were meant to name the world by discovering our Beloved's purpose for it. When they remove Him and His authority from this process, they end up listening to the unfaithful one or other foolish ideas, and create a fantasy world. As the material world does not care what these lost ones name it, it will help them see the foolishness of their fantasies and give them feedback through severe consequences to them. In essence, if they say one thing and do

something else, all trust is lost, and they will quickly destroy each other as a result.

This is similar to the above but needs to be said. If they have no sense of Our Beloved and His value; if they refuse to seek Him and his purposes for creation, their own value set will be distorted, bent and twisted. This will then twist their thinking and distort their lens or view of the world. As a result, they will have no sense of what is good, right or valuable and will make foolish choices because they have no value 'map' to guide them. A nation with distorted values is in a slow spiral of death unless they repent.

I am sorry these are more written out as points and not personalized to you. They are only notes written out to begin a conversation and get you thinking and asking questions with your new work ahead.

In the King's service,
Insight

Questions that would be relevant in your work.

Remember, these above areas are the fruit of sin, not the sin itself. You have to dig beneath the behaviour and get to the beliefs and values that are broken and out of sync with Our Beloved to truly deal with these issues.

What are the values and beliefs that are killing them through these actions?

How well is the Bride of Christ modeling our Beloved's heart to society?

Are they blaming society or finding ways to love them?

Insight@heaven.edu
Whisper@heaven.edu
Subject: Sovereignty of Our Beloved

Dear Whisper,

Let me finish by reference to the two foundations of their faith. As they struggle as individuals, families, churches and nations, they will need to constantly remind themselves and grow these two 'wings' of their faith in order to mature amid all the struggles of life in a dark world. Each honor bearer there must have them ingrained on their very hearts if they are to succeed and build a community that is worthy of our Beloved.

The first is that Our Beloved is BIG enough. They are muddled in their thinking about this area and honestly, they don't realize how important it is. Their world is a mess and they want someone to blame, and our Beloved is the easiest one because He does not defend Himself as they think He should. No matter what happens in their dark planet, the Sovereign One is BIG enough to deal with it.

Even when He has delegated authority to them, it is always, always in a context of His authority. And what He has asked of them, responsibility and stewardship, He will complete at His revelation on the final day. They have not seen the end of the story yet and only then will His Sovereignty be fully understood. Your honor bearer will always struggle with it in their dark world, but the victory is learning to trust in Our Beloved through faith in His greatness.

Our Beloved is GOOD enough. Our Beloved is love. Not in His nature, but in His character. It is a choice He makes rooted in the reality of His wisdom. Our Beloved wants a real, living relationship with them and has given them a choice to create life or death through their will. His love is extended to them in so many ways, and it is a mystery to me how many ways it has been misinterpreted and twisted. To keep your honor bearer on the straight path, always get him to keep his eyes on Jesus. That's how he will discover what Our Beloved's character is like. He is the perfect image of our Beloved.

How Big is their view of our Beloved?
How is their love and intimacy with
Him growing deeper and richer?

In the King's service,
Insight

Whisper@heaven.edu
Insight@heaven.edu
Subject: It's all about relationship

Dear Whisper,

Finally, I don't need to tell you how important
relationships are to our Beloved. We have
talked much about it in the above emails. In
His Kingdom they are intended for eternity.
For honor bearers to develop as a team, family,
community or nation, they must honor
relational ties. The relational values the
Almighty holds dear are embodied in these
ties. He created life and He expects all human
life is to be respected. Each one bears the image
of Our Beloved. He also created the physical
world in which they dwell. He intends their
relationship to His good Earth to be one of a
steward, not a devourer.

One last reminder, He gave them the authority
to name His created world. Words have great
creative power to define our relationships and
we are responsible for creating and
maintaining the meaning of them. The names
they use to define their world will define their
relationship to the world and each other.

Any name they use that takes them away from
Our Beloved's purposes or thinking destroys
them. This begins at a value level in the heart
and works its way into their thinking. Another
way of saying this is that if they give more or
less value to any object or if they think
differently about an object or life than Wisdom

does, then it becomes an idol. Idols are nothing more than a head stone to mark where they are dying.

Everything in their broken world is redeemable. Our Beloved is BIG enough to 're-create' any aspect of life in a way that good can come out of it. If there is something that has no redeeming value in it, then justice requires our Beloved to stop it and remove it. He has done these countless times, but our honor bearers will never know it.

You will be here soon, and I am full of anticipation in finally getting to catch up and hear all that is going on in and through you.

In the King's service,
Insight

Questions that would be relevant in your work.

How does humility play out in their relationships?

Where are their values out of sync or aligned with our Beloved's?

This will give you a sense where idols will easily develop.

How is the leaders' relationship with the poor, afflicted and those on the edge?

This will tell you how open they are to those who are different from them and their capacity to hold the pain of others. This is a key indicator in a leader's maturity.

About the Author

Matt Rawlins is CEO of Green Bench Consulting. He travels internationally as a trainer and consultant, dealing with leadership and organizational issues.

With a PhD in Communication, Matt has a heart to see people understand who they are and specifically, to help leaders communicate about difficult issues in times of change.

The author of 16 books, Matt is a gifted writer and communicator.

Matt currently resides with his wife Celia in Singapore.

You can contact him at: mrawlins@mac.com.

His business web site is: thegreenbench.com.